T 10223

SEA OF THE DEAD

ALSO BY JULIA DURANGO

THE WALLS OF CARTAGENA

SEA OF THE DEAD

Julia Durango

SIMON & SCHUSTER BOOKS FOR YOUNG READERS

NEW YORK   LONDON   TORONTO   SYDNEY

SIMON & SCHUSTER BOOKS FOR YOUNG READERS
An imprint of Simon & Schuster Children's Publishing Division
1230 Avenue of the Americas, New York, New York 10020
SIMON & SCHUSTER BOOKS FOR YOUNG READERS is a
trademark of Simon & Schuster, Inc.
For information about special discounts for bulk purchases, please contact Simon & Schuster Special Sales at 1-866-506-1949 or business@simonandschuster.com.
The Simon & Schuster Speakers Bureau can bring authors to your live event. For more information or to book an event, contact the Simon & Schuster Speakers Bureau at 1-866-248-3049 or visit our website at www.simonspeakers.com.
Book design by Chloë Foglia
The text for this book is set in Caslon.
Manufactured in the United States of America
2 4 6 8 10 9 7 5 3 1
Library of Congress Cataloging-in-Publication Data
Durango, Julia, 1967—
Sea of the Dead / Julia Durango.—1st ed.
p. cm.
Summary: When thirteen-year-old Kehl, fifth son of the Warrior Prince Amatec, is kidnapped by the Fallen King and forced to map the entire Carillon Empire, he also discovers a secret about his own past.
ISBN 978-1-4169-5778-2
ISBN 978-1-4169-9583-8 (eBook)
[1. Kidnapping—Fiction. 2. Cartography—Fiction. 3. Maps—Fiction. 4. Fantasy.] I. Title.
PZ7.D9315Se 2009
[Fic]—dc22
2009011410

For my father and his father before him,
who always loved an adventure;
and for my sons, who love them now

I KNOW HOW MEN IN EXILE
FEED ON DREAMS OF HOPE.

—Aeschylus, *Agamemnon*

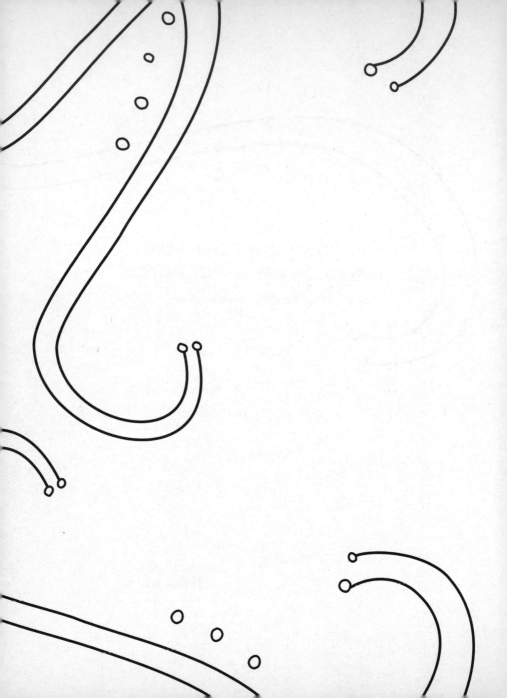

PROLOGUE

○ ○ ○ ○

IN THE DAYS before time, the Sun God Teshic had two wives: Malim, Goddess of the Lands, and Malim's sister, Carillon, Goddess of the Water. Though the sisters loved each other, their temperaments clashed like an axe to stone. While Malim submitted to her husband's authority, Carillon rebelled. While Malim was steady and predictable, Carillon was tempestuous and willful. And while Malim served her husband dutifully, Carillon ignored his commands.

Angered by Carillon's misbehavior, Teshic sent her a

warning: submit or be subdued. Carillon refused. "You are no more powerful than I or my sister. Why should we bow to you?" she said, unleashing a great tidal wave upon the Sun God. Furious, Teshic fought back and a mighty storm befell the world. Lightning cracked and thunder roared above the Lands and Water. The battle raged for days, until Teshic grew tired and ordered his wife Malim to join forces with him.

"No, sister!" cried Carillon. "Help me instead! Together we can break free of him!" she beseeched her sibling.

But Malim would not join her. "I will not defy my husband, even for you," she said, summoning the power of the Lands, which began to tremble and quake.

Though Carillon tried to fight back, she was no match for the combined strength of Teshic and Malim. Together they pushed her away. To reward his first wife's loyalty, Teshic gave Malim dominion over all the Lands' water: rivers, lakes, ponds, and streams. As for Carillon, she was exiled to the Deep, forever salting the water with her tears.

ONE

SWEAT POOLED IN my eyes and I wondered if this was what it felt like to be burned alive. Every muscle in my body screamed in agony and I fell to my knees, unable to take one more step. All I could think of was water. My throat was drier than dirt, like I'd swallowed handful after handful of finely ground cornmeal. Though my eyes were closed, I could feel my enemies draw near. A sharp stone hit my ribs, then another. Still I didn't move, thinking I'd rather be stoned to death than live another moment. It wasn't until someone spit in my face that I started forward again, crawling on all fours. I didn't need to look up to know the person who spit on me was my brother. No one else would dare.

An hour later I stood across from Master Yomatec, who'd summoned me to the archery range. He was alone when I arrived, letting loose one arrow after another into the target pit. *SWISH-THWACK! SWISH-THWACK! SWISH-THWACK!* Despite my fear and exhaustion, I couldn't help but admire the methodical rhythm of his movements. I'd spent endless hours over the past few years trying to mimic those same steps: pull arrow from quiver, nock, aim, release. It was the one martial skill I practiced with enthusiasm, for it didn't require an immediate opponent like hand-to-hand combat did. Rather, archery required a certain solitude of the mind, a kind of clarity I never felt with a knife or battle-ax in hand.

"You were a disappointment today, Kehl," Master Yomatec said, turning toward me after launching his final arrow.

Though I had prepared myself for punishment, his

words still caused my breath to catch and my stomach to knot. I held my head high and tried to keep my distress from the master.

"Your father is the mightiest warrior the Teshic Empire has ever known. Your four brothers passed through this military academy unequaled in skills, never once bested in combat by their fellow students. Now Vahl is our finest junior officer. He has made his father proud."

I swallowed hard and tried to speak forcefully. "I'm an excellent archer and the best cartographer in the school. I've heard you say so yourself, Master."

Master Yomatec raised an eyebrow. "That is so. You have a fine mind for detail and precision. But tell me, Kehl, how did those qualities help you run the Gauntlet today?"

I clenched my jaw in silence. The earlier torments of the day filled my head. Of all the torturous training forced upon us at the academy, the Gauntlet was by far the worst. For hours under the hottest sun we were made to run ten leagues with weighted packs strapped to us— through thick jungle, across rivers, up and down rocky terrain. The master's junior officers stationed themselves along the course, each with a bag of small, sharp stones. If any of us dared stop running, we'd feel their sting within seconds.

"At least I made it to the finish line," I finally said, trying to shake the memory from my head.

Master Yomatec narrowed his eyes. "You have Vahl to thank for that."

"Thank my brother?" I said, more loudly than I should have. "He spit in my face! He humiliated me in front of everyone."

Master Yomatec stepped closer, his big muscled body looming over me like a panther. "Vahl showed you your shame. He made you keep going when you were about to quit. Would you have preferred to fail?"

My face burned as I remembered crossing the finish line on my hands and knees like a dog. But I knew Master Yomatec was right. Failure would have been worse. My father would never have forgiven me, and that was a humiliation I couldn't bear. "No, sir," I said, looking down at my feet.

"You are dismissed, Kehl."

I bowed to Master Yomatec, then turned to make my way back to the garrison. Behind the imposing fortress I could see the sun, blood red, hovering over the endless waters of the Deep. Teshic had witnessed my shame. I would need to make an offering. I veered from the path and made my way to the stone temple of the Sun God.

While nowhere near the size or magnificence of the Golden Temple in the Lake City, the smaller garrison temple still boasted a towering statue of Teshic covered in gold, crystal, turquoise, and jade. I knelt at the altar and picked up a ceremonial knife. I pierced the palm of my hand and made a fist, letting my blood drip into the offering bowl.

TWO

VAHL WAS WAITING for me outside the temple, looking like the Sun God himself. Behind him I could see his slave, Jemli, limping hurriedly down the path, forever trying to keep up with my brother, who never did anything slowly.

"You have atoned?" Vahl asked me, crossing his arms over his massive chest. His golden wristbands glimmered in the setting sun, drawing attention to hard, strong arms, twice the width of my own. Beside him I felt like a child. I tried to remind myself that he was eighteen—five years older than I—and that I'd catch up to him in time. But part of me knew I'd never reach his level of perfection.

I lifted my hand to show him the bandage around my palm.

"Teshic does not suffer weaklings, Kehl. He will demand more than a few drops of blood if you continue to shame our family."

I dropped my head and gazed at the ground in front of me, blinking rapidly to ward off any angry tears that might humiliate me further.

Vahl looked around then at his slave, who had finally caught up to us. "And if you continue to slow me down, Jemli, it will be your heart that is sacrificed for Kehl's atonement. Understood?"

Jemli hung his head and stared at the ground as I did.

"Look at me and answer!" demanded Vahl, whose voice had become tight and dangerous. Jemli and I both snapped our heads up. I wasn't sure which one of us Vahl was talking to. Like all slaves of the military, Jemli's tongue had been cut out, to ensure he would never reveal our tactics to the Fallen.

"Yes, sir," I said, as Jemli let out a guttural sound of acquiescence. We both stood at tense, rigid attention, waiting for my brother to strike us.

Instead, Vahl waved a hand of dismissal at Jemli. "Tell the kitchen I'll be having a guest for dinner tonight."

Jemli made another raspy sound, then turned to limp back to the garrison as quickly as his scarred legs would carry him.

I continued to stand at attention, wondering if I would get off so easily.

Vahl smiled at me then and laid a hand on my shoulder. "Come, little brother. I think both of us are ready for this day to end, and I prefer to do so with good food in my belly. You will be my guest tonight in the dining room."

I let out a deep breath, relieved that his anger had dissipated. The officers had their own dining room with much grander fare than what we were served in the main hall. It was an honor to be invited to dine there, an honor my brother rarely bestowed on anyone, let alone me.

"Thank you, Vahl," I said gratefully, imagining the other boys' envy when they saw me in my brother's company.

My earlier embarrassment would now be erased. The Gauntlet would be forgotten.

"Listen to me," Vahl said, as if he knew what I was thinking. "You know why we push you harder than the others. You and I are the only two surviving sons of the Empire's greatest warrior. It is our duty to follow in Father's footsteps and one day lead the Emperor's Army. It's in our blood."

I looked down at the bandage on my hand. "But we share only Father's blood. Your mother comes from a warrior family. My mother was a commoner. Maybe that's why I'm not as strong as you."

Vahl looked at me sharply. "What's important about your mother's blood, Kehl, is that it was spilled by our enemies. Now you have vengeance in your veins, which is a powerful force. Let that vengeance be your guide, brother, and I promise you will become a great warrior. The Fallen will tremble at your feet and Teshic will reward you with power and glory, like he has our father."

I nodded in determination, fervently hoping my brother's words would one day prove true.

o o o o

When I finally fell asleep that night, I dreamed of my mother. It was the same dream as always, only this time something had changed.

It began in the usual way. My mother and I were walking along the beach, letting the warm water of the Carillon Sea tumble over our bare feet like frothy milk. Every now and then my mother would take my hand and give it a squeeze, and I would smile at her in return. That was all. The dream never changed, and I never wanted it to. For three years, ever since my mother died, I'd had the same dream. I'd come to think of it as a talisman—a blanket of protection my mother placed over me every night so I wouldn't be afraid.

Only this time, I *was* afraid. This time, my mother had stopped walking in the dream. Her face looked worried instead of peaceful, and the sea behind her no longer looked playful and gleaming, but dark and grim. She leaned down and placed her hands on either side of my face. "The time has come, Kehl," she said. "Be brave."

I had woken then, my heart pounding like a battle

drum. The room was dark aside from the faint sliver of moonlight shining through the window, barely illuminating the other boys in their beds. My classmates slept soundly, exhausted after a long day of the Gauntlet.

A slight scratching noise from outside caught my attention, and I looked toward the open window. A cat, perhaps, stalking its prey?

I shivered, though the night was warm. I couldn't help but wonder if my mother had been awakened like this the night she was murdered. Had she heard a sound too? Had she looked upon her killer as he climbed through the window?

I heard the sound again, and my skin prickled with fear. I thought about rousing one of the other boys, but quickly dismissed the idea. My classmates would tease me relentlessly were I to tell them about my dream, or wake them because of a small noise. And Vahl would have me whipped, no doubt, were he to find out. I took a deep breath, even as I heard the scratching sound a third time.

It's just an animal, I assured myself, rising slowly from

the bed. I walked toward the window, padding softly around my sleeping classmates.

When I reached the window, I stood and listened for a moment. Silence. A slight breeze blew in, bringing with it the scent of flowers. *Probably a tree branch scratching the outer wall,* I thought, leaning out the window to breathe in the fresh air.

At the same time, two shadowy hands reached out— one clamped over my mouth, the other around my wind-pipe—and disappeared with me into the darkness.

THREE

THE SMELL OF sea overpowered me and I struggled to orient myself. Stars glittered overhead and a crescent moon illuminated no more than shadows around me. My arms and legs were bound, and although I lay on a hard surface, I felt unsteady, as if the earth tumbled beneath me. Gradually I made out the shapes of tall beams draped with large expanses of cloth overhead, which blocked out the moon every time a gust of wind blew. The sound of waves filled my head, only instead of lapping gently on the shore, they were crashing into something hard. Something surrounding me.

Within a moment, my senses told me what I didn't want to believe.

I was at sea. Dead.

I had offended the Sun God and now I'd been sent to his enemy, Carillon, Goddess of the Deep. My life was over. No one ever went to sea—the graveyard of souls—and returned.

A human form moved in the distance and I called out weakly, my parched throat aching with effort. "Was my offering not enough? Why . . . ?"

The form moved toward me and I saw that it was a man, his head shaved clean but covered with black patterned markings. His facial features were as sharp as a battle-ax, giving him a fierce look that made me tremble even before I spied the knife in his hand. He gazed down at me with cold, hard eyes.

"You are a servant of Carillon?" I asked, wondering what wicked tortures lay in store for me.

The man smiled at that, showing off a mouthful of sharp, jagged teeth. "I am Mako. No man worships

Carillon more than I, but while I live and breathe I serve the Fallen King, no other."

My mind struggled to make sense of his words, but my head seemed shrouded in dense fog. "The Fallen King . . . ," I finally whispered. "Am I not dead, then?"

The man cackled, the moonlight glinting off his ghastly teeth, and I shuddered at the sight and sound of it.

"You may wish you were dead, boy, but no such luck. You're a prisoner of war aboard *Carillon's Revenge*, flagship of the Fallen. Your miserable life belongs to us now."

He raised a dark arm and let it swing, cracking me upon the head with his fist.

I slid back into darkness.

The next time I opened my eyes I saw daylight. The first glimmer of sun cast a pale pink aura in the sky. I was exactly where I'd been left—on the deck of a ship with my arms and legs bound—although from my position it was impossible to see water. Only the rocking movement of the ship and the occasional salty spray let me know I was indeed at sea. A prisoner at sea. A prisoner of the Fallen.

The thought made my heart pound. I was in the hands of my enemies. Like all sons and daughters of the Empire, I'd been raised to abhor the Fallen, who found ways to sneak into the Lands at night, raiding our weapons and supplies, and stealing our slaves to sacrifice to Carillon. After they murdered my mother, my abhorrence for the Fallen had turned to hatred.

Now I was their prisoner. But why? If they knew who I was they would have killed me, not kidnapped me. Had they mistaken me for a slave? Was I to be sacrificed to the Deep? My blood ran cold at the thought. I had to escape. I could not avenge my mother at the bottom of the sea. "Be brave," my mother had said to me in the dream. I did not want to fail her.

Little by little, I forced my mind to clear itself and recall only what was immediately relevant. I remembered my nightmare at the academy, the hand clapped over my mouth until all went black. They must have drugged me. How much time had passed since then? My stomach growled in answer: at least a day or two, maybe more.

I tested the ropes binding me, remembering what I'd been taught about the strength of various knots. They were tied expertly—not tight enough to harm me but certainly not loose enough for me to escape. I tried anyway, rubbing my wrists raw as I strained to pull them through the coils.

"My knife will free you momentarily. It will also gut you if you try anything stupid," said a deep voice behind me.

The voice's owner stepped into view and knelt beside me. He was a tall, well-built man with a handsome face, save for the long white scar that began at his forehead, skipped over his left eye socket, and ran down to his chin. The scar gleamed like a vein of silver against his dark skin. He wore his hair loose and his clothes were those of a commoner. Nonetheless, he had an imposing air about him that suggested authority. Ultimate authority.

"You are the Fallen King?" I asked, keeping my eyes on the quartz knife he held ready.

The man nodded. "That is what most choose to call

me. You may call me Temoc if you prefer."

"I prefer to call you *murderer*," I said, as the anger inside of me boiled over and drowned my fear.

"If my intent was murder, you'd be at the bottom of the Deep by now," he replied calmly, his razor-sharp knife slicing through the ropes around my ankles in two swift motions.

"I'm not talking about me," I said through gritted teeth. "I'm talking about my mother." I let my loosened feet fly then—one foot aiming for the knife, the other foot aiming for the king's royal nose.

FOUR

"YOUR AIM IS true, but you need to work on your speed," the Fallen King said after expertly dodging my feet and leaping behind me. He held his knife so closely against my throat I dared not breathe. "Stand up and look around you, young man, and I wager you'll not be so foolish again . . . at least not on my ship."

I did as I was told, slowly rising on wobbly legs, the king's knife held to my neck all the while. When I finally stood straight, he let the knife fall, knowing it was no longer necessary. In truth, the knife seemed a small danger compared to that which lay in front of me. Carillon. Sea of the Dead.

The blue stretched on forever, a watery otherworld of beasts and outcasts. No land in sight. Who but madmen would dare sail the Deep? Madmen and murderers. I turned back to the Fallen King, who now stood with a dozen men behind him, their knives, clubs, and axes drawn. They were a ragtag crew, dressed in common clothes like their leader, but their faces were as fierce as their weapons. Mako stood to the king's left, his teeth bared in a menacing grin.

"Do you understand your situation?" the Fallen King asked, his eyes narrowing as they scrutinized mine.

I understood perfectly. I was outnumbered, thirteen to one, with no chance of escape. I could die at the hands of the Fallen, or drown in the Deep. It was not a pleasant choice. My only hope was to play for time and wait for the odds to change. I nodded at the Fallen King.

"Very well. After you eat I will see you in my quarters straightaway," he said, then turned to his crew. "Xipi, report!" A short, spry crewman ran forward.

"Sir!"

"Feed this boy, then show him to my cabin," ordered the Fallen King, taking one last look at me before striding away.

Xipi motioned me to follow him. As I did so, I tried to take my bearings. It was hard not to marvel at the moving city around me. The only water vessels I'd seen before now had been the small poling boats and canoes we used on the lakes and rivers back home. Nothing like the massive structure I now stood on, its huge sails catching the wind like egret wings.

Several open stalls lined the middle of the deck, where the few crewmen who weren't tending to the complex sails were engaged in other tasks, like braiding rope and mending oars. Xipi stopped when we arrived at a stall lined with large baskets and hung with dried meats.

"You're lucky," he said, filling a small basket with fruit, corn cakes, and a variety of smoked fish. "We met with traders yesterday while you were snoring on deck."

My mouth watered at the sight of food, and I reached for the basket with my bound hands.

"No," said Xipi, moving the basket away from me. "Water first, so you don't choke." He pointed to a wooden barrel. "There's a ladle hanging off the side."

"Can't you take these ropes off me?" I asked, spilling water as I struggled to lift the ladle to my mouth.

Xipi shook his head. "Sorry, not without orders," he said, taking the ladle from my hands. He dipped it in the barrel again and held it to my lips. The water was cool and fresh and I gulped it down eagerly.

After I quenched my thirst, Xipi placed the basket of food in front of me and I devoured every last morsel, even the strange-tasting fishy bits. Xipi watched me with a curiosity that gave him a boyish appearance. In fact, the more I looked at him, the more I suspected he *was* a boy underneath his weathered face and scrawny frame.

"How old are you?" I asked, handing him the empty basket.

Xipi shrugged. "Eleven. Maybe twelve."

I stared at him in wonder. He was even younger than I. "How long have you been at sea? Were you kidnapped too?"

"Of course not," Xipi said. "I've been at sea my whole life, or at least it seems that way. Now come, Temoc will be waiting for you," he said, waving me out of the stall.

We walked to the rear of the ship where an enclosed cabin sat upon the upper deck.

"Do whatever he says and do it well," said Xipi, rapping on the door, then dashing away. I took a deep breath and braced myself.

"Enter," commanded a deep voice I now recognized.

I pushed the door open with my shoulder and let my eyes adjust to the dim light inside. The Fallen King sat behind a large wooden table with a stack of bark paper on it. A sleek gray dog sat at his feet, its head alert and ears perked at my arrival.

"Be seated," said the Fallen King, gesturing to the wooden chair across from him.

The dog growled and I hesitated.

"Sholla won't bite," the Fallen King said, rubbing the dog's neck. "Unless you forget your manners, of course." He smiled then, which altered the straight course of his scar into a fishhook along the side of his face. "I wouldn't dare try kicking her as you did me, unless you want to lose a foot."

"If you're waiting for me to apologize, I won't," I said, standing as tall as possible and lifting my chin. "I know I'm greatly outnumbered on this ship, and fighting you is futile. But you cannot stop me from thinking that you and your crew are godless thieves."

The Fallen King sighed, though he seemed more amused than dismayed. "You are just as I feared: stubborn, thickheaded, and blindly loyal to Teshic's golden Empire, tarnished as it is."

I struggled to keep my voice calm, though my heart pounded in my chest. "You would not dare speak of Teshic like that on the Lands. You'd be struck dead where you stood."

"Oh, I have dared," he said, waving a hand as if dismissing my words. "Have I not proof?" he asked, pointing to the scar on his face. "But your Empire will not be the death of me."

"You're dead already. Both the Sun God and the Earth Goddess have rejected you, just like they cast out Carillon."

The Fallen King paused. Sholla rested her head on his knee, and he reached down to scratch the smooth skin between her ears. "We are not dead, we are in exile, Carillon and I. Nor are we the only ones. And one day we shall return to the Lands, all of us."

"No one returns from the Deep," I said.

The Fallen King snorted. "I wonder what other lies Prince Amatec has told you?"

At that I could not help myself. My mouth dropped open like a little boy's.

He laughed at my amazement. "Did you believe we snatched you at random? Quite the opposite. I know exactly who you are, Kehl, fifth son of the Warrior Prince Amatec. And that is why you're here. I have a job for you."

FIVE

"SO YOU KNOW who I am, and who my father is." I could not keep my voice from shaking now, and I clenched my fists in anger. "And what of my mother? Do you know who *she* was? Do you know she was murdered in her sleep by the *Fallen*?"

"If I swear to you in Teshic's own name that the Fallen did not kill your mother, will you sit and let us talk like reasonable men?" the Fallen King asked, gesturing again toward the chair.

I shook my head. "You're a liar," I said, my hands aching

to break free of their ropes so I could squeeze the life out of the man in front of me. I now understood Vahl's words about the power of vengeance. It felt like there was an animal trapped inside of me, ready to spring. I wanted to kill this man, to make him pay for my mother's death and all the misery he and his lot had rained upon the Empire. But how? I had no weapon, and he dwarfed me in size. Even if I managed to get my hands around his throat, his dog would rip me to shreds. Outside his cabin the odds were even worse. Attacking him would be suicide, and I would die in vain.

"The Fallen did not kill your mother, Kehl," the Fallen King said again softly, breaking through my thoughts.

"Her throat was cut in the middle of the night! That is the mark of you Fallen, is it not?" I yelled, my eyes burning with rage. "Barbarians."

"No more barbaric than taking your enemies alive so you can cut out their hearts later." He gazed past me then, as if remembering something from long ago.

"That's different! It is an honor to be sacrificed on Teshic's altar. My mother was murdered in her bed!"

The Fallen King leaned across the table. "The Fallen did not kill her, Kehl."

"Then who did?" I demanded.

"In time I will tell you. But in return you must do me a service."

I hesitated then. *Was* he lying? I couldn't tell. What I did know was that my anger was making me reckless. I needed to focus again and keep to the plan: play for time and wait for the odds to change. It was my only hope.

"If it wasn't your people who killed her, how do you know who did?" I asked, forcing my voice to stay calm.

"Because it is my habit to seek truth . . . just the opposite of what they teach you on the Lands, is it not?"

"We have no need to *look* for truth. We obey our Emperor, who was chosen by Teshic to lead us. Teshic *is* the truth," I said.

The Fallen King reached down to scratch Sholla's ears again, a distracting habit I found at odds with his power. "You have much to learn, Kehl . . . and just as much to *un*learn."

I shook my head in exasperation. He gestured again

to the chair, and this time I sat in it, wearied by the exchange. "So what is the job you spoke of? What do you want from me?"

"I've heard you're a bright student," said the Fallen King, "and a talented cartographer as well. Is this true?"

I shrugged. It *was* true, or at least that's what everyone at the academy said. "I like maps," I finally answered, not sure how to respond.

"What do you like about them?" he asked, tilting his head in question.

No one had ever asked me about my interest in maps before, and I struggled to put my feelings into words. "I guess . . . I guess I like the possibilities they contain."

The Fallen King nodded. "And what are the possibilities you see in them?"

"I don't know . . . possibilities for the future, I suppose. Like where trade routes should be constructed or irrigation ditches or bridges . . . ," I said, trying to envision the maps I'd drawn at the academy.

"Go on," he said, as Sholla yawned and stretched herself across his feet.

"Or where to send your armies or how to divide your troops," I said, my words growing more confident now that I'd warmed up to the subject. "If you study a map long enough, a battle plan will eventually reveal itself, almost as if it had been waiting there all along, just for you to find it."

The Fallen King rapped his knuckles on the table, making Sholla bark beneath him. "Exactly. Which is why I need a mapmaker on board."

"Me?"

"You," he said, pointing a finger at me. "I want you to map the Carillon."

"That's impossible! Nobody's ever mapped the Deep. It can't be done."

"Why not?"

"Because we can't measure distance out here. On the Lands we measure by a man's pace, which is impossible at sea . . . or do you Fallen walk on water?"

The Fallen King laughed loudly, and for a brief second his eyes reminded me of my mother's, the way they'd crinkled in the corners whenever I'd made her laugh.

"No, my boy," he said, running a hand down his scar. "I'm afraid we Fallen are quite mortal beings."

I nearly smiled back at him, and had to remind myself that he was still my enemy, even if he hadn't killed my mother. "Then it can't be done," I said, crossing my arms over my chest.

"Oh, but it will, that is my charge to you," he said, his voice growing stern. "Find a way, and I shall tell you who murdered your mother."

"And if I can't?" I asked. Fear snaked into my voice, betraying me.

"Then I shall hand you over to Mako, my crew master. I believe you met him last night?"

I nodded, shuddering at the memory of his sharklike teeth and the brutal blow he'd given me.

"Then do we have an understanding, Kehl, newly acquired mapmaker of *Carillon's Revenge*?"

"Yes . . . your Kingship . . . sir," I said, tripping over my words, unsure of how to address him.

"I told you earlier my name was Temoc, did I not?" Though he spoke harshly, his eyes again were warm.

"Yes, your . . . Temoc."

The Fallen King raised one mocking eyebrow as I blushed furiously at my own foolishness. "Good. Now let me tell you the two immutable rules of my ship. One: Obey my orders under penalty of death. Two: In my absence, obey Mako under penalty of death."

I nodded, sitting so tensely in my chair that I jumped upon feeling Sholla's nose sniff my hands underneath the table.

"You may use my cabin to work. As you can see, I've plenty of paper and ink for you. But first I want you to ponder our dilemma of measuring distance, and how we might solve it. I look forward to hearing your thoughts."

"I'll try not to disappoint you," I said. And strangely enough, I meant it.

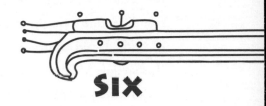

SIX

XIPI WAS WAITING for me when I left Temoc's quarters. "You're supposed to stick with me from now on," he said, as we headed back to the stalls. "Temoc says to make sure you don't do anything stupid, like try to make a swim for the Lands. I told him no one could be *that* stupid, not even a Landsmen . . . or are you?"

I was about to lob an insult in return when I saw him grinning at me, and I remembered his earlier kindness with the water. "Sure, you're brave now, while I have my hands bound," I said, "but wait until these ropes are cut and then I'll give you an answer you won't forget."

Xipi laughed. "Maybe you'd rather have Mako guard you? Let me call him," he said, putting two fingers in his mouth as if he were about to whistle.

"No!" I said, worried that he might actually do it. "Listen, just keep me out of Mako's way and I promise not to leave your side. Besides, I don't even know *how* to swim. If I jumped off this ship I'd sink like a stone."

Xipi looked surprised. "You truly can't swim?"

"I'm from the *Lands*, Xipi. What do you think?"

Xipi shrugged. "I've never been to the Lands. I've just heard about them from some of the men. Have you ever met the Emperor?"

I snorted. "Are you mad? The Emperor rarely leaves his palace. Only priests and princes of the Empire are allowed to see him."

"Like your father? Is it true he's the Warrior Prince? How big is his army?"

I held up a hand before he accosted me with more questions. "I'll make you a trade, Xipi. For every question I answer, I get to ask one of you in return."

"Agreed," he said. "So is it true—"

"But," I interrupted before he could say anything more, "first I need some time to think. As far away from Mako as possible," I added.

"I know just the place," said Xipi, motioning me back toward Temoc's quarters. He saw my hesitation and pointed to a rope ladder hanging from the side of the cabin. "Don't worry, we're not going *in*, we're going on top."

Xipi held the ladder for me as I fumbled my way up, once again cursing the ropes around my wrists. I hoisted myself onto the roof and inhaled sharply as soon as I saw the view. Carillon was beautiful and terrifying at the same time. The contrast of the brilliant turquoise water against the paler blue of the sky made me hold my breath as I contemplated the wonder of it. Somewhere beyond that blue was the end of the world. How could anyone measure such vastness? How could anyone map it? I let my breath out slowly, wondering where to begin such an inconceivable task.

"Are you wishing for home?" Xipi asked, interrupting my thoughts.

I had to think about my answer. "No," I finally said, surprising myself as much as Xipi. "I don't really have a home. Not anymore. For three years I've lived at the military academy at the North Garrison. Twice a year I visit my father in the Lake City." I shrugged. "There's not much to miss at the academy—just day after day of lessons and training."

Xipi nodded knowingly. "Sounds like Snakehead Island."

"What's Snakehead Island?" I asked.

Xipi hesitated, chewing on his lower lip. "I'm not sure I'm supposed to tell you."

"Why?" I asked, waving a hand at the endless sea and sky around us. "Because I might share the information with a seagull?"

"Exactly!" said Xipi, looking at me sternly. "How do I know the seagulls aren't working for the Empire? I wouldn't put it past those shifty birds. . . . Always making a racket, using our ship for a chamber pot whenever they please . . ."

I stared at Xipi, my eyebrows raised so high they must

have reached my hairline. I'm not sure who started laughing first, but I know I laughed longer and harder, until I had to wipe tears from my eyes. When I was done, I took a deep breath and my heart seemed to finally start beating at its normal pace—for the first time since I'd found myself on board.

"Laughing is always better than crying," said Xipi, looking like an old man again.

I nodded in agreement. "Now tell me about Snakehead Island," I said. "You owe me."

Xipi glanced around nervously, then spoke in a low voice. "It's where the troops train."

"What troops?" I settled back to listen, pulling my knees into my chin.

Xipi pointed a finger down at the roof. "*His* troops."

"And what does the Fallen King train his troops to do?" I asked. "Steal from the Emperor like wild dogs?"

"Ha!" cried Mako, springing up from behind us.

I gasped in pain as he grabbed a fistful of hair and snapped my head back.

"One cannot steal from a thief," he said, speaking

slowly between clenched teeth. "We will capture your Emperor and feed him bit by bit to the Deep. And then we will not *steal* but *reclaim* what is ours."

I winced as he jerked my head back once more.

"Teach him how to mend rope," he said to Xipi. Then he gave us each a shove that sent us tumbling off the roof.

SEVEN

LATER THAT AFTERNOON, Xipi and I sat sweating in one of the stalls, my fingers stripped raw from twisting, knotting, and braiding coarse rope fibers. Besides a few words of instruction, Xipi hadn't opened his mouth, nor had I. I was still aching from the bruises I'd received from my fall off the roof. Xipi winced every time he reached down for more rope, so I knew he was in similar pain.

Mako strode by us in regular intervals, watching my fumbling fingers with disdain. I almost felt like I was back at the academy, sweating nervously under the burning scrutiny of Master Yomatec or Vahl. I dared not say a word, but kept my head down and my hands moving. The Fallen King's second rule still echoed in my head: Obey Mako, under penalty of death. I had no doubt Mako would mete out my punishment with glee, were I to give him the slightest provocation. I did not intend to test him.

During the sun's descent to the eighth and final *q'or* of the day, the deck began to stir with activity. I looked at Xipi in question.

"We're about to land," he said. "Come with me."

We left the stall and went forward to the open deck, where Mako bellowed orders. His crewmen climbed through the rigging like monkeys, altering the triangular sails per Mako's commands.

"Sit there and stay out of the way," said Xipi, pointing to a barrel, then hoisting himself up a rope to join his mates above.

I sat on the barrel and gazed into the blue ahead of me. I finally spied the outline of an island in the distance. My blood ran cold despite the sun's warmth. I'd heard tell

of Carillon's islands; they were always described as uninhabitable, hideous crags of land made from the bones of
those sacrificed to Carillon. I shuddered and turned my
attention back to the crew. Who were these men who
chose to worship the Goddess of the Deep?

They were a strange and terrifying lot on the whole:
some old, some young, but all of them well-muscled and
nimble. Unlike my own embroidered red hip cloth, their
garments hung plain and white over sun-baked skin,
while simple leather slings held their tools and weapons. Most of them wore their long black hair in topknots
or braids, but a few shaved their heads entirely and had
facial markings like Mako's. And with the exception of
Xipi, all of them were heavily scarred, especially around
the legs.

It was this last detail that made me realize exactly
who they were.

Slaves.

Slaves from the Empire.

True, they looked stronger and fiercer than most of
the slaves on land, but the telltale scars were still there:

scars of the conquered. Throughout its rise to power, the Teshic Army fought to maim, not kill, aiming its storm of spears and arrows at enemy legs, not hearts. The dead were of no use to Teshic; the Sun God demanded slaves and sacrifices instead.

Xipi swung down from the rigging in front of me. He no longer appeared skinny to me, now that I'd seen him in action. His wiry frame was all muscle. "We're almost there. Look!"

I followed the direction of his pointing finger. The island appeared like a small green hill rising from the sea, covered with thick trees and vegetation. A white sandy beach ran along the perimeter, where small figures dotted the shore. It looked nothing like the barren wasteland I'd been expecting; on the contrary, it looked tranquil and pleasant. As we neared I noticed thatched roofs among the green, and I could now see that the small figures were people—men, women, and children—waving at the ship.

"Where *are* we?" I asked Xipi, who waved back at the crowd with both arms.

"White Cove Island," said Xipi, his eyes lit with

excitement. "Whenever we camp overnight here they make a huge feast for us. Then they play drums on the beach around a bonfire . . . the women sing and the men tell stories. . . . You're going to love it, Kehl, just wait!"

"Kehl is not to go ashore, Xipi," said Temoc from behind me, startling us both.

"Yes, sir," Xipi said, cutting me off just as I was about to ask "Why not?" From the look on Xipi's face, I understood that questioning Temoc would not be wise.

Temoc nodded at Xipi, then looked at me. Sholla stood by his side like a sentry. Though the dog's body remained tense and alert, her eager eyes gave her away: Xipi wasn't the only one excited to be going ashore. "Kehl, you will stay on board with Mako tonight," Temoc ordered. "Understood?"

"Yes, sir." Though I tried to stand straight, I felt my insides sink to the floor, wondering if I would survive to see morning.

As the crew lowered the four small canoes and rowed to shore, I watched the fiery-red sun sink into the horizon.

Teshic would be resting now, asleep in the strong, warm arms of Malim. I had always despised Carillon for her disobedience, but now as I leaned over the side of the ship, I pitied her loneliness.

The sound of drums carried over the waves and a chorus of voices rang out, echoing across the water. In the distance I could see a bonfire crackling along the beach, while shadows danced among the flames. A warm breeze brought with it the scent of roasted turkey, and I wondered if it was real or imagined.

In the moonlight I could see Mako sitting at the ship's bow, carving a piece of wood, his knife keeping rhythm with the drummers on shore. He had not spoken a word to me since the crew left, nor had he even looked my way. He seemed to relish the solitude, and I was glad not to disturb him.

I crept quietly back to the hammock Xipi had strung up for me on deck and let the steady beat of the drums carry me to sleep.

EIGHT

I WOKE IN THE night with a knife to my neck. Even in the darkness I knew it was Mako's face only inches from mine. My body froze with fright. I held my breath and closed my eyes, waiting for death. Temoc had lied. The Fallen had murdered my mother and now it was my turn.

"Whether you live or die makes little difference to me," he said slowly, his warm breath dampening my face. "But my king requires a service of you, and I will see it done. Betray him, and I will tear you to pieces as one day I will do to your father."

He yanked my arms up over my head and I braced myself for punishment. The tip of his knife slid from my neck to my heart, enough to scratch the surface of my skin. I opened my eyes then, wondering what torture would follow. His cold eyes gazed into mine and I flinched under their scrutiny. He seemed to be searching for something inside me, something he couldn't find. After what felt like an eternity, he raised his knife, cut through the ropes binding my wrists, and disappeared into the darkness.

I stayed in my hammock until the sun rose and I could wait no longer. I shuffled hurriedly to the side of the ship to relieve myself. In the distance I saw the crew launching their canoes off the beach. Someone must have whistled for Sholla, for she came bounding out of the trees and leaped into the last canoe.

I was glad to see them returning. After my run-in with Mako, the night had seemed endless, and though

I had ached to get up and stretch my newly freed arms,
I hadn't dared. Now that daylight had come and the rest
of the crew was in view, my fear abated and I stretched
my arms gratefully. My stomach rumbled as I did so, for
I'd been too afraid to make my way to the food stall the
night before.

Xipi did not disappoint me. He came climbing over
the side of the ship with a bulging bag strapped to his
back. It smelled of food.

"Let me help you with that," I said, reaching for
the bag.

Xipi grinned and handed it over. "You're very helpful
when you're hungry. Come on, let's go to the roof."

Once we were up top, I stuck my hand in the bag and
pulled out some corn cakes, still warm from the fire pit.
"So they grow corn on the island?" I asked in between
bites. "I didn't see any fields . . . unless they're behind all
the trees?"

Xipi shook his head, passing me a small flask of steaming *xocolat* he took from his hip belt. The spicy brown
liquid glided down my throat, awakening my insides with

its bitter heat. "They have small garden patches, but it's difficult to grow much on the islands," Xipi said, reaching for the flask and taking a sip of his own. "They get their corn, cacao, and other supplies from the Lands."

"You mean they steal it," I said, feeling vaguely guilty about the food I'd just wolfed down.

"Honestly, Kehl," said Xipi, making a face at me, "do you really think we're all thieves out here?"

I hesitated, trying to find a way to answer without offending him. "You're exiles. How else would you get things?" I said. "The Fallen aren't allowed to set foot on the Lands, much less buy from the markets."

"The Empire doesn't control *all* of the Lands, my friend, and traders abound out here," said Xipi, looking at me curiously as my eyes widened in amazement. "It's hard to believe that for all your training, you still know so little about the world."

I should have been angered by his words, and a day ago I might have been. I *would* have been. But I could not disagree with him now. The world as I knew it no longer existed. I watched Xipi peel a papaya and cut it open, revealing the round, black seeds inside. He handed me half of the fruit and we both settled back, juice dribbling down our arms as we devoured the flame-colored flesh and peppery seeds. I thought about all I'd discovered in just one day.

I had been taught that no one lived at sea besides the few evil, despicable men who chose to worship Carillon: marauders, thieves, murderers. The Fallen. Yet here was Xipi before me: a kinder boy than any I had known, who had just brought me warm corn cakes and *xocolat*.

I had been taught that the only islands at sea were uninhabitable, made from the bones of Carillon's victims and those sacrificed in her name. Yet within my eyesight was a lush island populated by men, women, and children.

I had been taught that the Fallen stole our slaves to sacrifice them to Carillon. Yet before me were a dozen men with telltale scars. The Empire's slaves were not being sacrificed, they were being recruited.

Did my father know? He had to. My father knew everything. The Emperor counted on him to know everything. I shook my head in confusion. "Xipi, I need to speak to Temoc."

At that same moment Mako barked out an order that could be heard even from our perch at the back of the ship.

"You'll have to wait, then. We're setting sail and you need to keep out of the way. You can request an audience once he's back in his quarters."

I watched Xipi skip off and stash his bag in the food stall before racing up a wooden spar to unleash its sail. Everyone had a job to do. Some, like Xipi, had their arms and legs wrapped around spars to lower sails, which fell like pleated curtains into the waiting hands of those below. Other men readied the steering oars. Still others heaved anchors up over the side. Every man worked hard. Every brow furrowed in concentration. Every back dripped sweat.

Besides Mako and Xipi, none of the crew had spoken to me since my arrival. I wondered if they'd been ordered to ignore me or if they simply had no use for me. Or worse, maybe they all despised me, like Mako did. I thought about what Mako had said to me last night: As long as I served Temoc, he would not kill me. I still had no idea how I'd ever map the Deep, but in the meantime, I could prove myself useful in other ways. Determined to show my worth, I propelled myself forward off the barrel.

WHAM!

The next thing I knew I was flat on my back, my head throbbing with pain. I'd jumped into a wooden spar just as it was swinging across the deck to be secured. A chorus of laughter filled the air.

"I suggest you go hide in my quarters, boy. The booms can't reach you there," said Temoc, standing over me with a grin. He offered a hand to pull me up, which I accepted, only because I was afraid I might fall down again were I to rise on my own.

This time it was I who avoided the eyes of the crew as I trudged to the back of the ship, holding a hand over the swelling lump on my forehead. The shame nearly ate me alive.

NINE

I TOOK THE LIBERTY of sitting once I reached Temoc's quarters, and rested my head upon his table. I closed my eyes and tried to block out the pain and embarrassment I'd caused myself on deck. My only consolation was that Vahl and my father had not borne witness to it. They would not have laughed at me as the crew had; they would have flayed me.

I felt the movement of the ship underneath me, and I knew we were under way. Moments later Temoc stepped in and I rose unsteadily from my chair.

"Sit back down and hold this on your head," he said, handing me a damp compress.

I wrinkled my nose. "This smells like a piss pot," I said, holding it away from me in disgust.

"Do it," he ordered.

I did as he said, using my free hand to plug my nose. I breathed through my mouth instead, but could still smell the acrid odor. Even Sholla backed away toward the window and whined until her master opened the shutters. Temoc himself seemed unaffected, though I daresay he might have been pretending such hardiness to make me feel small.

I unplugged my nose.

"It's not so bad once you get used to it, and it will keep the swelling down," he said, taking a seat across from me. "Now tell me, Kehl, why in Carillon's name did you leap off that barrel? Were you not told to stay out of the way?"

"Yes, sir," I said, hanging my head to hide the redness creeping up my cheeks. "I only meant to be of service. I felt useless sitting there while everyone else worked."

"I see. And how do you feel *now*?"

I did not need to look up to see the amusement on his face; I could hear it in his voice. My mother used to tease me in the same manner. "Like an idiot," I said, feeling my own mouth turn up in a rueful grin.

"If you want to help, Kehl, you can start by making that map." Temoc's tone had turned serious, and I looked up at him.

"But I've no idea where to start. . . . The Carillon is vast. . . . I still don't know how to measure it. . . ."

"Stop," Temoc said, holding up a hand. He took a piece of paper, quills, and ink from the shelf behind him and laid them in front of me. "Let's start with what you know. Draw me a map of the Lands."

"But—"

"Can you do it?"

I laid the compress down and nodded my head. "Yes. It will take some time, though."

Temoc stood. "Take what time you need. I prefer accuracy to speed. Come and find me when you're done." Sholla followed him out the door.

I stared at the paper in front of me. I'd drawn many maps of the Lands, but they'd always been copied. I'd never had to draw one from memory. I took a deep breath, then picked up a quill and dipped it in ink.

Several *q'ors* later, I rubbed my cramped fingers while Temoc inspected my work. I'd filled the square piece of bark paper from corner to corner, identifying major cities, roads, rivers, and mountain ranges. Tiny hash marks indicated distance by pace between the cities. The Emperor's Lake City sat in the middle, where I'd drawn a small picture of the Golden Temple. Small turrets represented the Empire's many garrisons, including three on the coastline that ran along the eastern edge of the map.

Temoc crossed his arms over his chest. "This is fine work, Kehl," he said, "but tell me something." He pulled a small dirk from his belt and ran it slowly around the edges of the paper. "What lies beyond the four sides of your map?"

I shrugged. "Wilderness to the north, west, and south. Carillon to the east," I said. "Nothing, really."

Temoc looked at me long and hard. "Nothing?"

"Well, the Emperor's scouts have reported scattered villages in the wilderness. Once the army reaches them, they'll become part of the Empire. The borders are always growing outward, at least on these three sides," I said, pointing to the landlocked edges.

"And these villages are nothing? The people who live in them are nothing?" he asked.

"They are of little consequence," I said, repeating what I'd heard my professors tell me. "They are an uncivilized people, useful only for hard labor."

Temoc narrowed his eyes. "Or sacrifice, I presume."

"That's right," I said. "It is an honor—"

"Yes, yes, it is an honor to be sacrificed to Teshic. Oh, how you Landsmen love to speak of *honor*," he said, his voice thick with anger. "But maybe we should go ask my crew for their opinions instead. Ask them how honored they felt upon seeing their fathers and mothers sacrificed. Ask them how proud they felt watching their sons and daughters slain upon Teshic's altar." Temoc raised his head in question. "Shall we ask them, Kehl?"

"No," I said, my heart pounding in my head. Until a day ago, I'd never heard anyone speak against the Empire, or even worse, against the Sun God. No one would dare. Temoc's defiance was terrifying and confusing at the same time. What kind of man would willingly pit himself against a god? Against Teshic himself? I had been raised to worship Teshic and defend the Empire. I had also been raised not to ask questions, and now my head swam with them. The lump on my forehead began throbbing again. "What does any of this have to do with the map?" I finally asked, reaching for the smelly compress.

"Everything. It has everything to do with the map, Kehl." Temoc strode to the door. "We'll meet here again tomorrow."

TEN

THAT NIGHT WE anchored off another island, but this time Xipi and most of the crew stayed on board. Only Temoc, Sholla, and two other men set off in a canoe for the island. Once they were gone, I accompanied Xipi to the food stall and helped him prepare rations for the men. Each man got a small basket of corn cakes, smoked fish, figs, and nuts. As I handed out the baskets, several of the men looked at me and nodded. I nodded back, trying not to reveal how pleased I felt by their recognition.

"Except for Mako, most of the men aren't too bad," Xipi said later as we sat on our perch above Temoc's cabin.

The men had finished eating and now sat in small groups here and there. A few, like Mako, sat by themselves, carving small pieces of wood in the moonlight.

"But why do some of them never speak? Have their tongues been removed?" I asked, thinking of my brother's slave, Jemli.

Xipi looked at me as if I were crazy, and I wondered how much he knew about slavery in the Lands. "Of course they have tongues, Kehl. Only there's not much for them to talk about. Their families and loved ones are all dead. They live quietly, work hard, and wait for the day they may avenge their people."

"Do they not fear Teshic?"

Xipi looked up at the sky. "When you've lost everything, there's nothing left to fear. Not even Teshic."

"So they worship Carillon instead?" I shivered at the thought. It was bad enough to ignore Teshic, but to side with his enemy? I could not imagine testing the Sun God in such a brazen, reckless way.

Xipi shrugged. "They respect Carillon, for she has given them safe haven. They respect the star deities for their guidance, especially out here in the Deep. They respect Elia, Goddess of the Moon, for the light she provides at night. But we have no temples out here, no altars, no priests."

I gazed up at the stars, trying to imagine such a life. The Golden Temple of the Sun God was the center of civilization on the Lands. We received our laws from the Temple Priests. We were ruled by an Emperor, divinely chosen by Teshic himself. "Without the gods, how do you know how to live?"

"Temoc says we must look to ourselves," Xipi said. A moment later he put a hand to his ear. "Listen."

From below us came the sad, hollow notes of a clay flute accompanied by a man's low voice, singing in a language I did not recognize.

"Those two are brothers, Six-Deer and Seven-Sparrow," said Xipi, pointing to the flute player and the singer beside him. "They're playing a remembrance song."

I shivered again, despite the warm breeze blowing across my back. Though I did not understand the words of their song, I felt the grief behind them.

"Their village was captured two years ago," explained Xipi. "Six-Deer was the only person to escape. Last year he and Temoc snuck into the Lands to free Six-Deer's family. Seven-Sparrow was the only one still alive. Their parents and sisters had already been sacrificed." Xipi laid his head back then and closed his eyes.

I did the same, and we both listened to the brothers' music. Never before had I considered slaves—the conquered—as people with their own lives, their own histories. Their duty was to serve Teshic's Empire, by the sweat of their labor or the sacrifice of their blood. But they were just like the rest of us—people with parents and children, memories and dreams. How could I have grown up without seeing that?

"And what of your family?" I asked Xipi once the music stopped.

"I don't remember them. I was a baby when the Empire's army attacked my village. My mother must have hidden me well, for I was left behind when they marched everyone out."

"Malim's heart!" I cried, raising myself up on my arms. "What happened then?"

Xipi smiled. "Temoc found me. Apparently I was bawling so loudly by that time he could hear me from the next village over. He took me to live on one of the islands at first, but every time he came to visit I would cry more and more loudly upon his departure. When I could finally speak, I begged him to let me live on *Carillon's Revenge* until I eventually wore him down." He laughed then, and I laughed with him.

It was hard not to like Xipi. All of the boys I'd been raised with—Vahl and my classmates at the academy— would never talk with me as he did. They would brag instead, or tell endless stories of their fathers' victories in battle. We were always competing against one another, always vying for position. It felt good to talk with some- one close to my age without feeling like I had to somehow win. With Xipi, I didn't feel like I had to prove myself, though I still wanted to.

"Tell me about your family now," he said.

I hesitated. "You already know who my father is."

"Amatec, the Warrior Prince. Mako told me." Xipi smiled wickedly. "He *hates* your father."

I snorted. "He doesn't like me any better."

"He doesn't like *anyone*," said Xipi. "But he especially hates the Empire's nobility. He thinks all twelve princes are mercenaries."

"Mercenaries? That's quite an insult, coming from a Fallen."

"I dare you to tell *him* that," said Xipi, tossing an acacia nut at my ribs. "Now tell me about your mother."

I'd been about to toss the nut back at him, but my arm fell and I looked away. "Her name was L'ezel."

"She passed on?"

I nodded. "Three years ago." My mother's wide smile and warm eyes appeared in my mind's eye.

"I'm sorry, Kehl. You don't have to tell me any more."

"I want to tell you," I said, and I meant it. Xipi had trusted me with his story. It was only fair I told him mine. "She was raised in a small northern village," I said, wishing now that I knew more about her life before I was born. Why hadn't I asked her when I had the chance? *Because you never thought about her being anything but your mother*, a voice inside of me answered. Shame licked me like a flame. "She was very beautiful and my father took her for his second wife. She and I lived on his coastal estate near the North Garrison. We were happy there." I smiled, remembering our walks on the beach. "My mother never liked the Lake City, although my father's palace there is quite grand. It's where my father's first wife lives. She had four sons—my brothers—though only the youngest still lives. I never met the others. They died in battle."

We were both quiet for a moment then, until Xipi's curiosity got the best of him. "And how did your mother die?"

"She was . . ." I blinked back hot tears and gave my head a shake. "Her throat was cut in the middle of the night."

Xipi looked at me, startled. "By whom?"

I closed my eyes then, trying to wash away the image of my mother's murder. I wanted to remember her walking on the beach, not covered in blood. "I don't know, Xipi. I don't know anything anymore."

We didn't speak after that, letting Carillon's gentle waves rock us to sleep where we lay.

ELEVEN

o o o o

THE NEXT MORNING I stayed on my perch while the rest of the crew readied the ship for sailing. I watched carefully, noting how each man went about his task. Although the rigging seemed quite complex, I thought I might be best suited for climbing masts and tending sails, like Xipi. Hoisting the anchors and turning the steering oars looked easier, but also required the most strength. As I was smaller than every man aboard save Xipi, the crew would likely laugh were I to offer my assistance with those tasks. I decided that later I would ask Xipi to teach me about the rigging.

A strong wind caught the sails and set us soaring. The Carillon glittered around us on all sides, her intense turquoise color offset by foamy peaks of brilliant white. Above us the sun burned bright and hot.

"Are you ready, then?" asked Temoc. He stood in front of the cabin door below, shading his eyes as he looked up at me.

"Yes, sir," I said, scrambling down the side, where Sholla greeted me with a nuzzle to the crotch. I pushed her away in embarrassment while Temoc snorted.

"What's hiding in your hip skirt, leftover figs?" he asked.

"No, just a few acacia nuts," I replied. Temoc let out a laugh, and I felt quite pleased with myself. He had laughed at me before, but almost always at my expense. This time we shared the joke and I liked it much better this way.

I followed him into the cabin with Sholla at my heels.

I gave her a scratch behind the ears, and she leaned her head to me for more.

Yesterday's map was just where we'd left it in the middle of the table. Across the top of it I'd written THE LANDS.

"The first thing I want you to do is change that title," said Temoc. "Erase 'Lands' please."

I did not question him. On the shelf behind us I found the necessary supplies and began to rub off the letters with a mixture of sand and oil. Once the word had been sanded off and the paper properly dried, I picked up a quill. "What would you like it to read instead?"

"The *Empire*," he said acidly, as if the word itself offended him.

I dutifully wrote the word, trying to keep my hand steady as Sholla plopped herself on top of my feet beneath the table.

Temoc placed a fresh piece of paper along the top edge of my map and another along the bottom. "Today we will begin mapping everything north and south of the Empire."

"But there's nothing there, remember?"

"*You* said there was nothing there. I did not."

I shook my head in confusion. "But I don't know what to draw. I've never seen a map of the wilderness."

"Because there *is* no map," he said. "You and I are going to create one."

I must have still looked confused, because he pointed to a stack of papers lying on a corner table. "Look," he said, pulling several pieces from the pile. "Here are all my notes and drawings about the northern and southern shorelines and the villages within. We're going to compile them and make maps to scale."

I looked through the papers he placed in front of me. They were covered with scribbles and blotches. I tilted my head about, trying to decipher the markings.

"I know, my writing skills are abominable. This paw is better suited for a spear than a quill," he said, flexing his large right hand. "But we will work together, Kehl. I will explain my notes to you, and you will draw the maps accordingly. Understood?"

"Understood," I said, intrigued by the challenge. After

my several embarrassments on deck, I was eager to prove my worth now. And the idea of mapping previously uncharted territories was thrilling. It meant I would have knowledge that even my professors at the academy did not have.

"Good. Let's get started, then," Temoc said, seating himself across from me. We leaned our heads forward and set to work.

TWELVE

FOR THE NEXT week my life fell into an agreeable routine. During the day I worked on the wilderness maps with Temoc. As we deciphered his notes, the maps slowly took shape under my quill. And though they were much less detailed than my map of the Empire, they were much more exciting to draw. Early on, Temoc explained to me that the land on either side of the Empire eventually turned inward toward the sea, like the tips of a crescent moon. So while the Empire's shore ran in a straight line from north to south, the northern and southern shorelines curved around until they were running west to east instead. As such, we were forced to add more paper until the pieced-together map filled the entire table.

After a week, we'd exhausted the notes. Although we had the general outline of both shorelines and a dozen villages plotted, our maps were still very sketchy and filled with guesswork. While Temoc's notes might reveal that one village was a full day's walk southwest from a certain estuary to the north, crossing a freshwater stream after three *q'ors*, we were still forced to speculate any number of details, such as which direction the estuary ran and whether or not the stream was a branch of it. I also had to estimate distance, since Temoc had only noted how long it took to get from one place to another rather than the leagues between them.

"It's a good enough start," Temoc said, "but now we must confirm what we've drawn and add more details."

"How?" I asked. "We've already gone through your notes several times over."

"We'll make a trip down the northern shoreline first,

then the southern. I'll talk to the villagers I know and show them the maps. They'll help us."

"May I go with you?" I asked, eager to see for myself the territory I'd just mapped. "I promise I won't run away, if that's what you're worried about."

Temoc raised his eyebrows. "Are you sure of that?" he asked, looking at me intently.

I hesitated. *Was* I sure? I no longer knew what I wanted. As much as I hated to admit it, I'd enjoyed the past several days on board more than any time I could remember since my mother died. "It would take me days to reach the Empire through unknown territory," I said haltingly, searching myself for an answer. "It would be foolish of me to even try."

Temoc shook his head. "Even if I believed you, Kehl, I'll have more than enough to do while I'm ashore than worry about you. Besides, I hear your lessons with Xipi are going quite well."

I nodded in agreement. Every evening before sunset we'd anchor at one of the many islands that sprinkled the Carillon like stepping stones in a pond. Temoc would row to the island with two crewmen and Sholla, while the rest of us stayed on board. Once Xipi and I served the dinner rations, Xipi would show me the various parts of the ship and explain how they worked. Oftentimes, some of the other crewmen would chime in, adding to Xipi's explanations with their own bits of knowledge and advice. After my lessons, Xipi and I would sling our hammocks near the food stall, frequently lulled to sleep by Six-Deer and Seven-Sparrow's music.

The more I learned, the more I was able to help, and the crew seemed to accept me for the most part. Mako still found every occasion to berate me when I made a mistake and scowled at me when our eyes met, something I tried to avoid whenever possible. But otherwise, I found myself enjoying my work with Temoc, my friendship with Xipi, and my new life at sea. Though I tried to remind myself that they were enemies of Teshic and therefore enemies of *mine*, the truth was I liked them.

"You and Xipi have both taught me a lot," I admitted. "I only wish my professors at the academy were half as interesting," I added.

Temoc laughed. "I'm sure it is no easy task to instruct a school full of arrogant, strong-willed boys. I might even feel sorry for your professors were they not teaching you absolute rubbish."

"It's not *all* rubbish," I said, feeling the need to defend the institution I had just criticized. It didn't seem fair for Temoc to judge what he didn't know. "They taught me how to make maps after all, which you've found very useful. And the combat instructors are among the finest warriors in the Empire," I added, thinking of Vahl.

"That may be true," Temoc conceded. "What I object to are the lies they feed you." The tone in his voice grew bitter as he put a fist down over the Golden Temple on our map. "They teach you to follow orders without hesitation, to conquer without question. To blindly obey your Emperor at all costs."

"How is that any different from what you demand of your crew?" I asked. "How is my loyalty to the Empire any different from your crew's loyalty to you?"

Temoc frowned. "I have earned my crew's loyalty by my own sweat and blood. Can your Emperor say the same?"

That gave me pause. The Emperor left the luxurious grounds of his Palace only to attend ceremonies at the Golden Temple. "I . . . I don't know," I said.

"Think on it," said Temoc, as he put away our quills and ink for the day.

THIRTEEN

A FEW DAYS LATER *Carillon's Revenge*
lay anchored in a small cove along the northern shoreline.
As usual, Temoc rowed to shore with two crewmen and
Sholla, leaving the rest of us behind; only this time he
would be gone for three full days instead of one night.

"They're recruiting more villagers," said Xipi, as we
watched the canoe grow smaller in the distance. "Soon
there'll be enough of us to take on the Empire!"

Before drawing the map with Temoc, I might have
snorted at Xipi's suggestion. The Empire's army was five

thousand men strong. But now I knew something the Emperor didn't: He was surrounded on three sides by quickly growing rebel armies. And if those three sides joined forces, they'd become the Empire's deadliest foe in generations. For a brief moment I fantasized about escaping the ship and returning to the Lands to warn them of the danger. I would be a hero! I imagined the look of envy in Vahl's eyes as the Emperor placed a circlet of gold upon my head. . . .

"Oof!" I spluttered, as a bucket of cold water splashed the back of my head.

"Hey!" cried Xipi, as he got doused from the other side.

We both turned indignantly to face our attackers. The entire crew stood behind us, laughing. Six-Deer and Seven-Sparrow were up front, swinging empty buckets in their hands.

"You smell like rotten fish," yelled Mako. "Wash yourselves, or we'll do it for you!"

Xipi and I did not need to discuss the matter. We shook ourselves off and made haste for the stern.

"Let's take a canoe around the cove," Xipi suggested after we had thoroughly scrubbed our hip cloths, hair, and bodies with a barrel of fresh water. "The sea creatures out here are amazing."

"All right. As long as they are *small* sea creatures, and not the kind that will eat us," I said. I'd seen shark fins cutting the water several times since coming aboard the ship, and I was not eager to see one up close.

Xipi laughed. "Don't worry. Your hair will more than likely scare away any sharks who dare tip their noses up for a peek."

I flipped my wet head at Xipi and splashed him with droplets, then ran my fingers through my knotted hair until it was smooth and untangled. It had grown wild and unruly since my days at the academy, where we were expected to keep our hair groomed neatly. The sun had bleached all the dye from my hip cloth and baked my honey-colored skin to the dark brown of my crewmates. I looked more like a Fallen than a prince's son, and I wondered if anyone I knew on the Lands would recognize me now. I pulled a piece of string out of the pocket of my hip skirt and tied my hair back so it wouldn't stick to my face or neck. The sun was brutally hot, and without the sea breeze that kept us cool while sailing, I was already beginning to sweat.

Xipi and I lowered a canoe and set off under Mako's strict orders to stay within sight of the ship. We rowed lazily. We were in no hurry, nor did we have any wish to exert ourselves. Within moments we were floating in water so clear we could see the sand at the bottom. Fish of all shapes, sizes, and colors darted here and there, and we took turns pointing out our favorites. Every now and then we'd spy a fat manatee somersaulting in the distance.

"Have you ever seen anything like it, Kehl?" Xipi dragged his fingers through the water and wiggled them every now and then, causing the brilliantly hued fish to scatter in all directions.

I shook my head. "I've lived by the shore my whole life, but I was always forbidden to go in the sea. Although sometimes my mother and I would sneak away from the house slaves and tutors and walk along the beach."

"House slaves and tutors! That must have been nice."

"Nice? Hardly. They never left us alone. From the time we woke up until we went to bed at night, they were always hovering over us. I used to get angry with them, but my mother said it wasn't their fault. They were under strict orders from my father to look after us."

"Did your father visit often?"

"Once a month he traveled to the North Garrison to give the men their orders from the Emperor. The officers would come to our house and my father would host big feasts in our courtyard, where they'd drink maguey wine and share news." I scooped up a handful of water and poured it down the back of my neck to cool off. My father's monthly visits were not a pleasant memory. I remembered how eager I was to please him, and his inevitable disappointment when I failed to measure up to my older brothers' accomplishments.

Xipi made a face. "Maguey wine. Yuck. Temoc forbids wine on board, but lets the men drink their fill of it on the islands now and then. I tried it once and got so sick I retched for days."

"I did the same once, and I swear I'll never take a drink of it again. My father always made my mother pour the wine during his feasts so he could show her off to the men. I hid behind the courtyard plants once and drank from the men's cups when they weren't looking. My mother found me throwing up in her flower beds a few hours later."

"Ha! Did she whip you for it?"

"No, she cleaned me up and helped me to bed. Then the next morning for breakfast she brought me a huge cup of wine. I thought I was going to throw up all over again just from the smell of it," I said, laughing at the memory. "'Have you had enough then?' my mother said, waving the cup under my nose. She loved to tease me like that. She said she liked it best when I learned lessons from my own mistakes."

"She sounds like the kind of mother I'd like," said Xipi, smiling, then frowning a moment later. "Why would anyone want to kill her, Kehl? Who would do such a thing?"

We both sat silent for a while, staring into the water.

"My father says the Fallen killed her," I finally said, looking into Xipi's eyes.

"The Fallen!" he said, his brow furrowed in disbelief. "They would never kill a woman. Soldiers, yes. Guards, yes. But never a woman. Never someone's mother!"

"My father says they did it to punish him," I said.

Xipi shook his head. "No. They wouldn't do that, Kehl. I promise you. Your father's mistaken. Or else he's . . ." Xipi looked away from me.

"Or else he's *what?*" I asked, not sure I wanted to hear the answer.

Xipi slowly turned his eyes back to me. "Or else he's lying to you, Kehl."

"My father wouldn't lie to me," I said firmly, as much to reassure myself as to convince Xipi. "At least not intentionally. But Temoc knows who did it," I said, "and as soon as I find out, I will avenge my mother . . . even if I die trying."

I picked up my oar and began to row back to the ship then. Xipi did the same, and for the rest of the day we didn't speak.

FOURTEEN

BY THE TIME Temoc returned a few days later, *Carillon's Revenge* sat gleaming in the bay. The crew had reinforced the sails and pitched the seams, while Xipi and I had mopped the deck from stem to stern. He and I had fallen back into an easy camaraderie, though we limited our conversation to banter and jokes. The topic of mothers, fathers, and the Fallen was now a sore subject for us—or at least for me—and I did not wish to burden Xipi with it.

Once we set sail, Temoc summoned me to his quarters. "We have work to do, Kehl."

The northern villagers had answered many of our questions about the map, and we set about making the necessary additions and changes. After a few days, our map had improved enormously, although the added details to the north only accentuated the vast empty portion to the west and the sketchy area to the south.

"Soon we will travel to the southern shoreline to fill in this part," said Temoc, pointing to the bottom of the map. "But for now, let us set our sights here." He circled the empty area between the shorelines. The Carillon. "Though we haven't yet determined how to represent distance at sea, we might as well add what islands we can, even if their locations aren't accurate."

"But I may know a way we can represent distance," I said hesitantly. "I've been thinking about the way you and the crew never use physical measurements to describe distance like we do on the Lands. You use time instead."

Temoc ran a palm down the scar on his face and nodded thoughtfully. "Go on."

"Instead of saying 'Village One is twenty-six hundred paces or half a league from Village Two,' you say 'Village

One is four *q'ors* or a half day's walk from Village Two.'"

"Yes, that is true...."

"So rather than indicating paces and leagues on our map of the Carillon, why not indicate *q'ors*—the time it takes to sail from one place to the other—instead?"

Temoc leaned over our map, gazing at it as if it might hold some answers for him. "I like your idea, Kehl. But what of bad weather? You haven't yet experienced a storm at sea, or high winds, or no winds at all. Any one of those things might easily double our normal sailing time."

"Are the winds predictable more often than not?" I asked.

Temoc tilted his head to the side, considering my question. "For the most part, yes," he said. "There are some seasonal variations, but those are fairly predictable as well. After thirteen years at sea, one begins to recognize its patterns."

"So we'll note the distance by *q'ors* under normal sailing conditions. That's the best we can do. Anyone using the map will have to mentally calculate adjustments based on the weather. But at least they'll know *where* the next island will be, even if it takes them a bit longer to reach it."

Temoc passed me a quill. "Let's do it."

For the next ten days, Temoc and I spent hours laboring over our map, trying to pinpoint the exact location of each island. I soon learned that a dozen major islands stretched across the Carillon like a snake from north to south. Each of these islands had a name, which I added to our map in neat, tiny symbols. We also added the twenty or so smaller islands surrounding the chain, and symbols to indicate villages, freshwater sources, protected inlets, shallow waters, dangerous reefs, and other details we thought useful. Rather than the hash marks I'd used to denote leagues on land, I drew small spirals to represent *q'ors*, the eight units of time on a sunstone between sunrise and sunset.

Our work was aided by our journey. Temoc had instructed the crew to sail down the chain of islands, stopping at each one. At night he showed our map to the islanders and asked for their assistance to fill in various details.

"Our island friends are impressed by your skills, Kehl," he told me one morning upon his return. "It gives them hope to see that the Empire is only one sixth of our map, and to see we have allies to the north and south. Your map has done much to convince people that the Empire is not nearly as invincible as your Emperor believes."

"But by this time next year the Empire will have conquered two more slices of land to the north and south," I said flippantly. "And were the Emperor to see this map, he would immediately call his armies to march down the shorelines in both directions to keep you from conspiring with your allies on land."

Temoc's head snapped up and his eyes pierced me like arrows. I immediately regretted my words. "But the Emperor will *not* see this map, will he, Kehl." It was not a question, but an order.

"No, sir," I said, turning away from the scrutiny in his gaze.

FIFTEEN

WHITE COVE ISLAND was the eleventh island in the chain, and Xipi complained bitterly when Temoc told us the crew would not be going ashore.

"But they always have a feast for us! We'll disappoint them if we don't show up," Xipi said, trying to plead his case with Temoc.

Temoc laughed and rubbed Xipi's head none too gently. "We're a large group to feed and I don't like to take advantage of their generosity. Besides, I want to get an early start so we can make it to Snakehead by dusk tomorrow."

As it was, we arrived at Snakehead even earlier, due to a strong wind that seemed to fly us there. At first view, Snakehead Island looked much like the other islands in the chain—a lush, green hill rising out of the sea—only larger. But it wasn't until the crew sailed us around to the eastern side of the island that I saw what made it special. I gasped in amazement. Six ships as grand as *Carillon's Revenge* sat anchored in the island's wide bay. A score of smaller sailboats, longboats, and canoes bobbed among them. On shore, hundreds of men moved about, framing the hulls of three more large ships.

Xipi hopped excitedly beside me at the bow. "It's the fleet, Kehl! Isn't it spectacular? And look up there!"

My eyes followed his pointing finger. Above the shipbuilders I could see rows of archery ranges and fighting pits. It reminded me of the academy, and for a moment, I wondered if anyone there missed me.

Xipi's voice broke through my thoughts. "The men here learn how to fight *and* sail. Temoc says I can come here in a year to learn how to fight. By that time, I could probably *teach* the classes on sailing," he said, slapping the bowsprit proudly.

I stood quietly beside him, still awestruck by the sight and overwhelmed by what it meant. The Empire had nothing more than three garrisons to guard its coastline, preferring to station the bulk of its defenses along the landlocked borders instead; after all, the Carillon had posed no threat to them in the past, save occasional raids by the Fallen. The fleet in front of me could easily over-run any one of those coastline garrisons. Even if the fleet were to arrive in the light of day, alerting a garrison to an upcoming attack, it would take days for inland army reinforcements to travel to the coast. By that time, the garrison would be taken. "Who are all those men, Xipi?" I asked, watching them move about like ants on the shore.

"Escaped slaves, volunteers, villagers who abandoned their settlements as the Empire neared . . . and there are women here too. Mostly they help build the ships and make weapons, but some of them train alongside the men."

My mouth dropped open and Xipi continued, even

more animated than before. "It's true, Kehl. The best archer on Snakehead Island is a woman! Her name is Zemah. Temoc invited her on board once, and the crew nearly fell over themselves, she was so ferocious and pretty at the same time."

I laughed at that, and we spent the rest of the evening on our perch above Temoc's cabin, watching stars and imagining ourselves to be great warriors.

The next day we began our journey to the southern shoreline. When we were less than a *q'or's* distance away, clouds scuttled across the sky and soon the Carillon's calm blue water turned choppy and gray. Every man quickly took to his station as Temoc shouted orders, trying to keep the ship on course. The wind buffeted our sails, and my insides somersaulted as the ship bucked and weaved. I felt the contents of my stomach rise in my throat and I stumbled across the deck, hoping to get to the side before I vomited.

"Inside my cabin, Kehl, now!" Temoc yelled from the bow. "Use a bucket if need be, but don't come out until I tell you!"

"Yes, sir," I muttered, though I doubt he heard me in the wind. I tripped down the deck and fell into the cabin, where Sholla greeted me anxiously. I grabbed a bucket and heaved into it several times until my body ran dry. Then I curled up in a corner with Sholla and prayed to every god I knew of—even Carillon, *especially* Carillon—to see us safely to shore.

When Temoc finally summoned me back on deck, we were anchored off the southern coast, the land barely visible in the dark night. The storm had abated, but not before causing considerable damage to our masts and sails. The men looked exhausted.

"We'll all go ashore tonight," Temoc said. "Tomorrow we'll assess the damage and make our repairs during the light of day." He walked off toward his cabin, carefully stepping his way through the fallen wreckage. "Mako, prepare the canoes."

Sixteen

○ ○ ○ ○

MY MIND RACED with conflicting feelings as we neared the shore. After three weeks at sea, I would finally be back on the Lands. If I wanted an opportunity to escape, now would be my chance. I might not be able to swim, but I certainly could run. But did I want to? What would greet me back at the garrison? A hero's welcome for escaping, or punishment for letting myself be kidnapped? Surely if I told them about Temoc's map, I would be lauded . . . or would they blame me for helping him?

"Come on, Kehl, grab my hand and follow me," said Xipi.

We'd made it to shore. My legs felt oddly unsteady as I climbed out of the canoe and started walking up the beach. Xipi helped me try to keep my balance. "The same thing happens to all of us after being at sea," he said. "Just keep walking and soon enough you'll have your land legs back."

I did as he said and followed the rest of the men up the shore. Temoc and Sholla had already gone ahead to alert the nearby villagers of our arrival. Mako led the rest of us through a thick copse of palm trees, lighting the way with a torch. Within minutes we arrived at the village, a small settlement of wooden huts and thatch lean-tos. The buildings circled a common area where a bonfire crackled, warming the cool, damp night. A dozen men sat around the fire with Temoc, smoking tobacco pipes. They stood in quiet greeting as we entered the clearing.

While our crew joined the others by the fire, Temoc signaled for Xipi and me to stay where we were. "One of the families here has generously offered to let you sleep in their hut tonight," he said. "Go there now and settle in. I'll see that dinner is brought to you."

"But—," Xipi and I said in unison, equally distressed by the news.

Temoc put up a hand to silence us. "You will do as I say."

"Yes, sir," we murmured, understanding the conversation to be over.

Half a *q'or* later we sat in our borrowed hut, still grumbling about being treated like babies. Earlier a white-haired woman had brought us savory bowls of turtle stew; now a skinny young man entered with two cups of steaming *xocolat*. "For our guests from the sea," he said, smiling at our appreciative faces. His voice broke when he spoke, and though he was taller than I, I guessed him to be about my age.

"Thank you," I said, as he handed me a cup. "I am Kehl, and this is Xipi. We appreciate your hospitality."

"I am Okemli," he said, handing the second cup to Xipi. "My brother and I live here with our grandmother.

It is an honor for us to host the Fallen King's crew."

Xipi and I both took big swallows of the hot, bitter brew, warming our hands on the cups as the liquid warmed our insides.

"Are the men still talking out there?" Xipi asked, while Okemli waited for us to finish.

"Yes, like old women!" he answered, flapping his hands together like turkey beaks. Xipi and I laughed. "You're better off in here, where you can rest."

Xipi yawned loudly. "I *am* sleepy," he said.

Okemli nodded knowingly. "It's my grandmother's stew," he said. "It puts me to sleep too."

Moments later, Xipi was snoring soundly.

Okemli walked over to him and waved a hand in front of his face. Xipi didn't budge. "He's out for the night," Okemli said, turning to me. "We can talk now."

I looked at him in surprise. "About what?"

Okemli's eyes lit with excitement. "About your escape!" he whispered.

I sat up straight, my weariness gone. "What do you mean?"

"You're Prince Amatec's son, right?"

"Yes . . . how did you . . . ?" I could barely speak for my astonishment.

"My brother overheard two of your crewmen talking about it. Do you know your father's offered a reward for your return?" I stared at the boy as he continued. "My brother will come for us as soon as the men are asleep. Then we must be ready to run."

My heart pounded in my head. I did not want to leave, but guilt overcame me. I had a duty to my father. This might be my only chance. I looked over at my friend, Xipi.

"Don't worry about him," said Okemli. "I put sleeping powder in his *xocolat*. He won't wake for hours."

I cringed. I hated for Xipi to think that I had deceived him. He had been my first true friend, and now I was abandoning him. I only hoped he wouldn't be blamed for my escape.

While Okemli packed three rucksacks with food and water, I paced the floor of the small hut until another young man appeared silently in the doorway. In the candlelight, I could see he looked just like Okemli, only older.

"Let's go," he whispered, and the three of us disappeared into the night.

Our journey over the next three days made the Gauntlet seem like child's play. We could not walk along the shoreline for fear of being followed by Temoc's men; instead we zig-zagged through thick jungle, barely speaking as sweat soaked our bodies like rain. Okemli's brother, Bahna, kept us going at a fast pace, covering our tracks as we barreled through the heavy vegetation. Every now and then, Okemli would try to strike up a conversation with me, but the journey was much too arduous for more than a few words. Our meager provisions went fast, and by the third day we were hungry, exhausted, and covered with insect bites. After we'd made camp that night, I fell in a heap, waiting for sleep to put me out of my misery.

Even as I felt the first rays of dawn against my eyelids the next morning, my body refused to move, pleading for a few more moments of rest. I tried to go back to sleep, but the sound of hushed voices kept me awake.

"We'll reach the South Garrison today," said Bahna. "Where shall we go once we claim our reward, little brother?"

"Let's go inland to the Lake City. I've always wanted to see it. They say it's filled with golden temples and jeweled palaces . . . gardens that stretch for leagues, and markets overflowing with anything your heart desires. We could buy a house for grandmother there!"

"We could buy a palace if I sell Amatec some information along with his son."

"What information?" Okemli asked.

"The Fallen King plans to raid the South Garrison during the next half moon. That's only a week away. I heard him ask four of our villagers to accompany him."

Though alarmed by his words, I forced myself to stay still so I could keep listening.

"What are they going to do? What are they after?" asked Okemli.

"Weapons for the rebel army," Bahna said. "I believe such information would fetch a good price from the Warrior Prince, don't you?"

"But we'd be betraying our own people! They'd be slaughtered!"

"Your heart is too soft, Okemli."

"And yours is too dark. I won't do it!"

"We'll see about that," Bahna said.

I heard Okemli wince under his brother's blow.

My eyes flew open then and I sat up. "What's going on?" I asked, glaring at Bahna.

"Nothing," he said, glaring back at me. "Now get moving. We're almost there and I'm half-starving. I hope your slaves know how to cook," he added, slicing through the vines in front of him.

I looked back at Okemli. A purple bruise swelled on his cheek, and tears glistened in his eyes. "Are you all right?" I asked.

"I'm fine," he said, trying to smile at me through his pain. "We're almost there, Kehl. You're almost home!"

Home. I did not have the heart to tell him that the word was meaningless to me. It was my duty I was returning to, not my home.

SEVENTEEN

LEAGUES BEFORE WE reached the
South Garrison, sentries spotted us and sounded the
alarm. The garrison's commanding officer met us as we
emerged from the trees and onto the beach.

"State your business," he demanded, his men behind
him armed with spears.

"My brother and I are here for our reward," Bahna
said, pushing me forward. "Here's your prince."

The officer looked at me in disgust, taking in my dirty
hair, insect-covered body, and filthy hip-cloth.

"I am Kehl, son of Amatec," I said. "I was kidnapped by the Fallen. These brothers helped me escape."

The officer continued to study me with distaste. "Throw those two in the dungeon," he finally said, pointing to Bahna and Okemli. "Take this one to the garrison. I'll summon Amatec from the Lake City."

They did not let me leave my room at the garrison for five days. Though I pleaded with my guards to release Okemli and Bahna from the dungeon, or to at least let me visit them, my pleas fell on deaf ears. They were under orders from my father to keep all of us locked up until his arrival.

My room at the garrison was nothing more than a stark soldier's cell, but I was grateful for a bed and the porridge, corncakes, and fresh water delivered every day. Slowly I regained my strength, sleeping for hours and hours on end. When I wasn't sleeping, I was thinking, a storm of thoughts rolling in and out of my head like crashing waves.

What would I tell my father?

I was his son. It was my duty to tell him everything. Vahl would not hesitate in my position. By now Vahl would have also alerted the garrison guards to the upcoming raid. From what I'd overheard Bahna say, the raid would take place in just a few days' time. Maybe Bahna had already told the guards. Then what? I must tell my father everything I knew, for he was sure to find out anyway.

But each time I resolved to tell the truth, I would remember my crewmates—Xipi, Six-Deer, Seven-Sparrow. In a few short weeks they had become my friends. And Temoc. He had sworn to tell me who killed my mother. Would the knowledge die with him, when my father's men were sure to ambush the raiding party? Could I let that happen? No. And so I would resolve to tell my father nothing, hoping Bahna would do the same.

After going back and forth like this any number of times, pacing my room in a frenzy, I would go back to my bed and sleep some more, my only escape from the war inside my head.

○ ○ ○ ○

When my father finally arrived on the sixth day, he did not come to my room. Instead, he had me summoned to his personal quarters. I stood quietly in the doorway, dazed by the opulence in front of me. Embroidered tapestries hung from the walls, while the floor was covered in the finest ceramic tiles. Sculptures lined the room, carved with scenes of battle and sacrifice. The dining table could not be seen underneath all the plates and dishes on it, piled high with delicacies. My father sat before the feast, ripping the meat off a roasted iguana leg. A serving slave cleared his throat to alert him of my arrival.

"Son!" My father rose to embrace me as I entered the room. The jade and turquoise stones of his gold breastplate pressed uncomfortably into my skin. He pushed me back from him and frowned at my appearance. "Malim's heart, Kehl, you look like an outlaw. Have a slave cut your hair and bathe you tonight. I can barely stand to look at you."

I nodded, feeling small and stupid, the way I always did around my father. Though we shared the same dark eyes and prominent chins, there was never any way to please him, no way to measure up.

"Eat with me, you're all skin and bones," he said, returning to his chair. "Three days I've been traveling from the Lake City and I'm ravenous." He bit into a cassava cake and motioned for me to sit down. "Now tell me everything."

I hesitated, still unsure of myself. Did I tell him everything? Nothing? Something in between? I needed to know if Bahna had told him about the upcoming raid. Half moon was tomorrow night. "Have you spoken yet with the two brothers who brought me here?"

My father nodded. "I paid them a visit as I came in, although one was already dead."

My stomach turned over. "Dead? How—?"

"I'm told the older one tried to escape two days ago. Had a run-in with the guard," he said, ripping more meat off the iguana carcass, "and *lost*," he added with a laugh.

So Bahna was dead. How could he have been so foolish? "And what about the other one?" I asked, worried about Okemli. "Has he left yet? Did he claim his reward?"

"He tried."

"What do you mean?" I asked, growing nervous by my father's tone.

"Would you have a stupid boy squander my money, Kehl? *Our* money? He was a commoner with no one to miss him."

I felt my face go pale. "You had him killed?"

"Yes, and you will concern yourself with it no longer," my father said, signaling a hovering slave to pour him more wine.

I clenched my teeth in anger. It was difficult to even look at my father now. Okemli and Bahna were dead. Though I may have cursed them for their interference during these past few days, I had never wished them dead. I had liked Okemli, even if his brutish older brother reminded me of Vahl; maybe I'd liked Okemli even more because of it.

"Now tell me what Temoc's up to," my father said. "They say he was your captor." Though he kept his tone casual, I shivered under his icy gaze. My father was testing me, and we both knew it.

"You know who Temoc is?" I asked, quickly trying to gather my thoughts.

"Of course. The Fallen King, leader of fallen men and cowards. Did he tell you I gave him that scar on his face?"

I shook my head dumbly.

"And what of Mako?" my father asked. "Is he still alive or is that shark at the bottom of the Deep by now?"

"Mako's still alive. But how do you know them, Father?"

"They were both warrior chiefs years ago, from villages up where the Northern Garrison now stands. They banded together when our army came, but still they could not defeat us. I should have killed them both on the battlefield. Instead I sent them to the Lake City to be sacrificed. They escaped."

My head spun. Temoc and Mako had both fought my father. And lost. No wonder Mako hated me. And Temoc? Did he hate me also? Had he kidnapped me to seek revenge on my father?

"So what did they want *you* for, Kehl?" my father

asked, wondering the same thing I was. He pushed a plate of smoked game toward me, but I felt too nauseous to eat anything, particularly meat.

I shook my head. "I don't know. To punish you, I guess."

"Did they ask you questions about me? Questions about the Empire?"

"No. Nothing specific," I lied, thinking about the map I'd made for them. The map locating all the Empire's forts and garrisons. The map they might one day use to attack my father's army. A drop of sweat rolled down the back of my neck.

"Then what did they have you do this past month? Braid their hair?" Though my father joked, I could hear the cold suspicion in his voice.

"No, sir. They kept me tied up the whole time. Maybe . . . maybe they knew you would eventually offer a reward. Perhaps they were going to have someone turn me in for the money."

"Perhaps," said my father, his brow furrowed. He signaled for more wine.

We sat in silence for a moment as my father gazed at me. One of the serving slaves came forward and nervously filled his cup. The slave's legs were scarred and I tried not to look at them, sure my every glance and gesture would give me away. I picked up a fig and took a bite so my mouth would not betray me.

"Did they say anything about your mother?" my father finally asked, his eyes narrowing as I shifted uncomfortably in my seat.

"No," I said. "Nothing at all. Did they know my mother?" I asked, trying to keep my voice calm, though my heart pumped so furiously in my chest I was afraid he might hear it.

My father did not answer. Instead he dismissed me with a wave of his hand. "You may go."

EIGHTEEN

I TOSSED AND TURNED all night,
unable to sleep. The next morning I walked down to the
beach, now that I was no longer a prisoner in my room.
The Carillon was calm and still, like a blue blanket. I
found a piece of deadwood to sit on and let the tide run
over my feet and ankles. Gulls wheeled overhead while
I stared at the horizon. *Carillon's Revenge* was out there
somewhere. Somewhere close, perhaps, though I could
not see it.

Tonight was half moon, the night of the raid. Would

Temoc and his men succeed or would they walk into a trap? I still did not know if Bahna had revealed their plans before he died. But I knew I could not let them be slaughtered like Okemli. . . . Okemli, who had stood up to his brother, refusing to betray his people for money . . . Okemli, who had been murdered, betrayed by my father after doing him a service.

I sat there for hours until my skin burned under Teshic's bloodred sun. I walked into the Carillon up to my neck, letting the water cool me. I held my breath and dunked my head, feeling my hair float around me like seaweed.

The sun was setting by the time I returned to the South Garrison. I quietly made my way to the dining hall and stopped in front of the closed doors. Deep voices rumbled within. A harried-looking slave came out, a tray piled high with empty dishes in his hands. Once he was out of sight, I peered inside. My father and the garrison officers sat around the table.

"What was the Fallen King doing in the southern

wilderness to begin with?" asked a young officer, reaching for a tray of candied fruits.

"The brothers who brought Kehl here said his ship was caught in a storm. He and his crew were forced to land and stumbled across the village," answered the oldest at the table, his topknot streaked gray and decorated with feathers to signify his rank.

"And how did the villagers—or at least the boys who brought him here—know about Kehl's kidnapping and the reward?"

"They said a trader from another village told them."

"But how did the trader know? How did news from the Empire leak out to the wilderness?" asked the young officer.

"I'll tell you how," my father said quietly from the head of the table, looking around at each man. "Spies. Our borders have been infiltrated."

"Then perhaps it's time for another war of expansion," the young officer said, pounding the table for emphasis. "To the south this time!"

My father cleared his throat and the men fell silent.

"I've already sent a messenger to the Emperor. The army will mobilize here in a fortnight's time. My son, Vahl, will lead them."

The officers raised their cups and began to voice their approval. My father lifted a hand to quiet them again. "I do not believe the Fallen King's presence there was an accident. I want every village burned to the ground in punishment for harboring the Fallen. And if the Fallen King is found among them, I want him taken prisoner and given to *me*." He raised his own cup then, and the other men followed suit. "He took L'ezel from me first, and then he tried to take my son. I will see him skinned alive," he said before taking a long, slow drink from his cup.

The flesh on my arms rose. So Temoc had killed my mother. He had lied to me.

"Pardon me, sir," a voice whispered behind me.

I jumped in surprise. The slave had returned, his tray laden with more food and wine. I opened the door for him, careful not to let myself be seen by the men inside. Then I dashed for the armory.

NINETEEN

MOMENTS LATER I crept toward the shore, using the darkness and palm trees to keep me hidden from the sentries atop the garrison tower. In one hand I held a spear, pointing it to the ground so that its quartz tip would not shine in the half moonlight and give me away. Around my shoulders I wore a leather holster sheathing a knife made of pure obsidian. I was the Warrior Prince's son; the armory guard had not questioned me when I took the weapons from his store. Though I'd longed to take one of the gleaming longbows and a quiver of arrows, I'd made myself select more practical weapons. The night ahead would call for hand-to-hand combat, not distance.

I did not go all the way down to the beach, but continued along the tree line instead. They would come from the south, by canoe rather than land, to provide a hasty retreat if needed; no soldier of the Empire would dare pursue them into the Deep. I made my way to the estuary half a league's distance from the garrison and waited among the tall reeds. From my location I could see the mouth of the river feeding into the sea: the perfect place for a landing party to leave their canoes and sneak ashore. I settled in and stared into the darkness.

When I finally saw two shadows glide up the river, I nodded to myself in satisfaction. I'd calculated correctly. I held my breath and waited while they secured both canoes, then watched them walk toward me. Six men approached. Temoc and Mako, plus four I didn't recognize—the men from Okemli's village. Knives and axes gleamed from holsters around their shoulders, waists, and legs as they snuck up the shoreline.

When they were no more than ten paces from my location, I summoned my courage and called out the Fallen King's name. "Temoc!"

The other men froze and reached for their weapons, but Temoc recognized my voice and ran toward me. "Kehl! Are you—"

I raised my spear and aimed it at his heart. He stopped short, his eyes staring into mine. He was no more than five paces away. I cocked my arm back and readied my spear.

Behind him the other five men raised their knives and axes.

"Lower your weapons, men," said Temoc without taking his eyes off me. The men hesitated. "Do it!" he yelled.

Everyone did so but Mako. "I knew he'd betray us," he yelled, raising his ax higher. "Slithering back to his father like a traitorous snake."

"That's not true," I yelled back at him, standing my ground. "I may have left, but I didn't betray you," I said, my eyes returning to Temoc. "You betrayed *me*."

"Stand down, Mako," Temoc ordered. Mako did as

he was told and sheathed his ax, but his body remained tense and coiled like a viper, ready to strike. "Kehl?" Temoc asked, waiting for me to explain myself.

"You lied to me!" I said. "You said you didn't know my mother, but you did!" Though my voice shook, my hand remained steady around the spear.

"I did not lie to you, Kehl. I never said I didn't know your mother. I said I didn't murder her."

"But you did kill her! I heard my father say so!"

"Your father lied. She was my sister, Kehl."

I stood frozen, trying to comprehend his words. "Your sister . . . but that means . . ."

WHOOSH! A glinting object whistled past my ear.

Temoc fell to his knees before me, the ornate handle of a throwing knife protruding from his right shoulder. I whirled around and saw my father emerge from the darkness. Ten armed guards appeared behind him, their spears raised.

"Your mother was a spy, Kehl. A traitor to the Empire," my father said as his guards fanned out, surrounding Temoc's men.

"*You* killed her?" I cried. "You killed my mother . . . your *wife?*"

"She was a spy for the Fallen. She deserved to be publicly drawn and quartered. Only for the sake of our family name did I show mercy and kill her quickly. Now show me your loyalty, son, as your mother did not: Join me, and the Empire shall know you as a hero for leading us to the Fallen King!"

TWENTY

I STOOD ROOTED TO the spot as if
Malim herself had planted me there. I was caught between
two circles. Behind me Temoc's men had formed themselves into a small shield around their wounded leader.
They stood with their backs to one another, in order to
better defend themselves against the larger surrounding
circle of my father and his soldiers. Every weapon was
raised for battle. Every man was ready to strike.

"Come, Kehl!" my father yelled.

"No!" I cried, stepping backward to join the smaller

circle, then bracing myself for the onslaught. Those of us in the middle were outnumbered eleven to seven, with one man already wounded. It would be over quickly.

My father looked furious. He cocked his spear. His men did the same.

SWISH-THWACK! SWISH-THWACK! Two arrows flew out of the darkness, racing toward their targets. Two of my father's men fell to the ground as the copper-tipped arrows shot through their hearts, killing them instantly.

SWISH-THWACK! SWISH-THWACK! Two more soldiers fell as arrows pierced through their necks and out the other side. Blood splattered upon my face and I tried not to gag.

In the blink of an eye, the battle had evened. Seven to seven.

My father roared in fury, and the two sides rushed each other like wild boars. Six-Deer and Seven-Sparrow came running out of the shadows to join the fray, having exchanged their bows for knives. Seven to nine, our favor now.

I dropped my spear and drew my knife for close

combat. Behind me Temoc struggled to pull the throwing knife from his shoulder. I stood in front of him like a guard, though my father's men did not approach us. They were leaving us for my father, no doubt.

Screams of pain rang out, punctuated by the clash of weapons. I forced myself to keep my eyes on the battle around me, though I wished to close them tight. My father had engaged two of the villagers, but I knew by the confident sneer on his face that they were no match for him. He dodged their every blow, taunting their failed attempts. A moment later he swung his knife in one wide arc, cutting both men down as he pivoted in the sand.

And then he turned his sights on us.

Temoc had wrenched the throwing knife from his shoulder and now stood ready, his own knife unsheathed. "Run, Kehl," he whispered, his voice tight with pain. "You know where the canoes are. Take one and row south. Go!"

"Not without you," I said, feeling my breath catch as my father strode toward me, his knife dripping blood.

"Move aside, Kehl," my father demanded.

"No." I raised my knife, willing my knees not to buckle underneath me.

My father's eyes cut mine like glass. The next second he picked up my fallen spear and cracked me across the head with the wooden shaft.

When I opened my eyes next, I saw nothing but red. I wiped the blood out of my eyes and struggled to lift my head. I counted nine men still standing. Six-Deer and Seven-Sparrow each fought a soldier. Mako fought two. And my father fought Temoc, whose shoulder wound now bled freely, staining the sand around them. He would not last long. I scrambled to my feet just as Temoc fell to his knees again, barely conscious.

"No!" I cried, throwing myself in front of Temoc as my father raised his knife. "Father, please!"

"You think I will spare you because you're my son?" he spat, the knife trembling in his hand. "I still have another son, Kehl. A warrior son! But you ... you are a traitor, just like your filthy mother."

His knife plunged toward me and I braced myself for death.

But just as the knife was a breath away from my neck, an ax came hurtling through the air, cleaving my father's heart in two. His eyes opened wide, not in pain but in disbelief, as if shocked by his own mortality. I almost pitied him.

That is all I remember.

TWENTY-ONE

o o o o

"IT MUST HAVE been a pleasant dream," Xipi said, as I opened my eyes. "You were smiling . . . for a few moments, at least."

I nodded, still half-asleep. "It was the old dream where my mother and I walk the shore and the sea is calm. The one where she squeezes my hand and I know everything is okay. I didn't think I'd ever have that dream again." I closed my eyes and tried to go back to it.

"Do you know where you are, Kehl?" Xipi asked, shaking my arm.

I opened my eyes again and let them travel around the small, familiar room while I slowly inhaled the salty air. Sholla lay curled at my feet. "Temoc's cabin." I was back aboard *Carillon's Revenge*. My head throbbed and I reached up to determine the source of the pain. My entire skull was bandaged.

"Ten stitches it took to sew your head back together," said Xipi, pulling my hand away from the bandage. "Better leave it alone so it can heal. That was quite a blow you took."

Memories of the battle came roaring back to me. "Where's Temoc?" I tried to sit up, my heart beating in quick panicked bursts. "Where's Six-Deer and—"

Xipi gently pushed me back down onto the makeshift cot I'd been lying in. "Careful, Kehl. I'll tell you everything if you promise to lie still and rest your head."

I'd made myself dizzy by my sudden movement. I could not have stood if I wanted to. I sank back into the cot and closed my eyes. "I promise. Now tell me."

Xipi wiped my face with a cool compress as he spoke. "Temoc, Six-Deer, and Seven-Sparrow are all out on deck. They each have new scars to add to their old ones, but otherwise they're fine."

I breathed a sigh of relief. I would never forgive myself had they been killed due to my own foolishness. I should have known I would be followed. I should have known my father would not let me out of his sight so easily.

"I'm sure all three of them will be in shortly," Xipi continued. "They keep coming in like mother birds, even though I've promised to let them know as soon as you're awake." I could hear the old mischief in Xipi's voice, and it warmed me. "But since you're still only half-awake, they can wait a few minutes longer."

"And Mako?" I asked. "I suppose he's out there sharpening his blade, cursing the day I came aboard and wishing he'd finished me off while he had the chance."

"Ah," said Xipi and then went quiet.

I opened my eyes. "Xipi?"

"I think I'd best call Temoc now. He'll want to see you," he said, rising from the floor next to me. He took my hand and pressed it between his. "I'm glad you're back home, Kehl."

o o o o

Temoc entered quietly. He walked with a slight limp and his shoulder wound was wrapped in linen. Though he tried to smile, his eyes betrayed his grief.

"Mako is dead?" I asked, already knowing the answer.

Temoc nodded slowly, then lowered himself beside me, careful not to split the stitches running across his left knee. "You must forgive him, Kehl. He was not always such a hard man."

I raised my eyebrows in surprise. I could not imagine Mako being anything but fierce and heartless.

"He was once a brave and noble man who loved a young woman, and dreamed of the day he would marry her. That woman was my sister, L'ezel. But then the Empire came and took everything he loved away from him, including her. She was forced to marry someone else and bear someone else's son. And then she was murdered. After that, he lived only to avenge her."

"My mother . . . ," I whispered, trying to imagine my mother's life before she married my father. Before she had *me*. A whole life I knew nothing about. "Why didn't she ever tell me about you? She should have told me!"

"You were too young, Kehl. L'ezel wanted to protect you, at least until you were old enough to make your own decisions. She wanted to keep you safe."

"But what about her own safety? She spied for you and was murdered for it!"

Temoc's head dropped and he rubbed his eyes with a tired hand. "We begged her to leave your father, to come with us and live on the islands. She insisted that she was more useful to us on the Lands. And that she would not subject her son to a life of exile—unless he chose it for himself."

"How could I choose something I knew nothing about?" I asked, squeezing my eyes shut to keep the tears inside.

"She would have told you, Kehl, had she lived. But you were still a boy when she died. After her death, Mako and I respected her wishes. But the day you turned thirteen, we resolved to wait no longer. He and I kidnapped you together."

"But why didn't you tell me all this before?"

"We did not know you, Kehl. We didn't know if we could trust you. You were raised in the Lands. We needed time to understand the kind of person you were."

"And what was your conclusion? That I was unworthy of your trust? Mako almost *killed* me last night!"

"Mako died for you last night, Kehl. It was his ax that killed your father. As soon as he let it go, he left himself unarmed against two soldiers."

Though I tried to hold them back, tears ran down my cheeks. I wasn't even sure who I was crying for— my mother, my father, Mako, myself? All of us, perhaps. Temoc brushed my tears away with the back of his hand.

"There were times when you reminded me of my mother," I said, trying to steady my voice. "Now I know why."

Temoc smiled and placed a hand on my heart. "You are much like her, nephew."

"I hope so," I said, putting my own hand over his. "Shall we bring down the Empire now?"

My uncle's eyes gleamed. "Why don't we take a look at our map first."

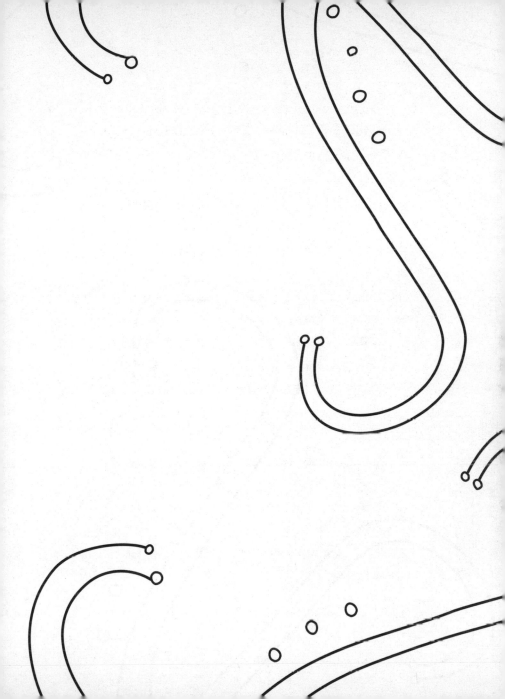

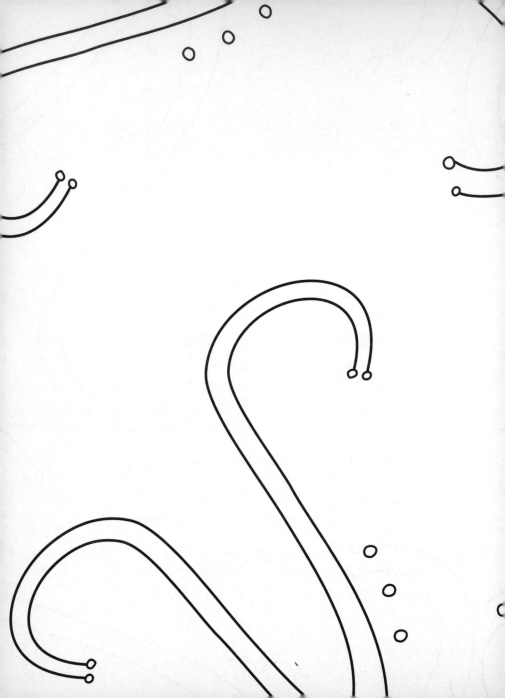

o o AUTHOR'S NOTE o o

Though *Sea of the Dead* is entirely fictional, it was greatly inspired by my interest in pre-conquest Mexico and the Caribbean Basin. The initial story seed arose from several "what if" questions: What if the Europeans had never arrived in the Americas? What if the Aztec Empire had continued to expand its territories? What if that expansion eventually reached the shores of the Caribbean? What if the conquered nations took exile at sea?

Obviously, these events did *not* occur, making my story pure fantasy. The Teshic Empire never existed. And while certain details of the setting were influenced by preconquest history and the Caribbean landscape, nothing in the story should be taken as fact. Instead, I highly recommend the following books to fellow history enthusiasts:

Aguilar-Moreno, Manuel. *Handbook to Life in the Aztec World.* New York: Oxford University Press, 2006.

Josephy Jr., Alvin M. *America in 1492: The World of the Indian Peoples Before the Arrival of Columbus.* New York: Knopf, 1992.

Mann, Charles C. *1491: New Revelations of the Americas Before Columbus.* New York: Knopf, 2005.

o ACKNOWLEDGMENTS o

Heartfelt thanks to the trinity of writing superheroes in my life who made this book possible: Kevin Lewis, my editor; Barry Goldblatt, my agent; and Tracie Vaughn Zimmer, my writing partner, who shared every page of this adventure with me. Thanks also to the wonderful talent at Simon & Schuster Books for Young Readers; Team Barry; the Silly Chicks; McKinley School staff and students; and my Ottawa writing pals for ongoing support and camaraderie.

Finally and most important, I would like to thank my family and friends, who make my small corner of the universe the best place to call home.